MYSTERY OF THE BRASS-BOUND TRUNK

From the moment Nancy Drew boards an ocean liner leaving for New York, she becomes involved in a new and dangerous mystery. A man on the pier gestures to someone on board in the sign language of the deaf. BEWARE OF NANCY DREW AND NE, he signals. Who is NE? Can it be Nelda Detweiler, a young South African who shares a cabin with Nancy, Bess, and George? When Nancy learns that Nelda has been accused of stealing a diamond bracelet in South Africa, she wonders whether the girl is a thief or the innocent victim of a vicious plot.

Then an unclaimed brass-bound trunk, delivered to Nancy's cabin by mistake shortly after she embarks, becomes the first clue that leads her to believe international jewel thieves are aboard. And soon afterwards she realizes that her life and the lives of her friends are in danger. Mystery and intrigue follow the girls across the ocean; but with her usual ingenuity Nancy solves the mystery and defeats her enemies before the ship reaches New York.

"Nancy and Nelda, we want to question you about a theft," the FBI man said.

NANCY DREW MYSTERY STORIES

Mystery of the Brass-Bound Trunk

BY CAROLYN KEENE

GROSSET & DUNLAP
Publishers • New York

Contents

Mystery
of the
Brass-Bound Trunk

CHAPTER I

Two N.D.'s

"All visitors ashore!" shouted a steward. All visitors a—!"

As the call to leave the *Winschoten* faded away in the distance, there was a hum of excitement on the ocean-going vessel. Bells were ringing and the ship's horn was bellowing out short blasts.

"Good-by! *Tot ziens!*" passengers called to those on the pier.

Three attractive girls stood together, leaning on the rail and watching the people onshore, who were waving. One was Nancy Drew, a strawberry blond who had sparkling blue eyes. On her right stood pretty Bess Marvin, a slightly plump blond, while on her left was Bess's cousin, a slender, athletic girl who enjoyed her boyish name, George Fayne.

The three girls were about to sail from Rotterdam in Holland to New York City. Along with other passengers they waved and shouted good-by to those on the pier, although they knew no one.

Suddenly Nancy's attention was directed toward a man on the dock. He was using the sign language for the deaf and finger spelling a message to someone on the ship. His hat was pulled low so that she could not distinguish his face.

Nancy watched his fingers move quickly; she was fascinated. Then, in a moment, she was startled to see him spell out the words NANCY DREW. Two years before, Nancy had learned the entire finger alphabet but had forgotten most of the letters except those that spelled out her own name. "How strange," Nancy thought. "What does he mean by that?"

Bess and George were looking in other directions and did not notice the man. Nancy kept trying to figure out the rest of his message.

After a short pause, he started again. Deciphering the letters she did know, Nancy pieced out part of a sentence. It read: —EWARE NANCY DREW AND NE— She could not decipher the last part because her view was obstructed by someone.

Nancy, an amateur sleuth, looked up the deck to see if she could find anyone on board who was signaling in the finger language. She noticed no one, because the crowd of people along the rail blocked her view. Curious to solve the puzzle, Nancy leaned far out over the rail and turned to gaze along it, hoping to get a glimpse of someone spelling out words. Without warning, she felt her feet slipping and her balance going. She tried to steady herself, but could not. She would fall into the ocean below!

Bess turned to Nancy just in time to notice that her friend was in trouble. With a great yank, she pulled the girl back. "What were you trying to do?" Bess asked. "You gave me a terrible scare."

Nancy smiled ruefully. "That was silly of me. But a man on dock was talking to someone on board in the deaf sign language and he signaled a warning about me!"

"What!" George and Bess exclaimed, taken aback.

"Where is he?" George asked.

Nancy looked toward the spot where the man had been. "Oh," she said, disappointed. "He's gone now."

"What are you going to do?" Bess asked.

"Well, if he talked to more than one person, the others might still be conversing in the finger language. Maybe we can find them."

George spoke. "You don't even know which deck these people might be on. If you really want to find out, I suggest we split up and do a little sleuthing."

"Good idea," Nancy agreed. "Suppose I stay here. Bess, you take the lower deck, and George, you go to the one above. If there are two or more deaf people together, they might still be speaking in the finger language. I'd like to know whom the man on the dock was talking to."

Bess and George hurried off, while Nancy continued to look around for suspects. She saw no one and kept thinking about the words she had translated. She was not on a case. Why should anyone be told to beware of her? And what did NE stand for?

As she pondered this question, the girl detective kept a sharp watch on her fellow travelers, who were waving and calling out to those on the pier. Most of the people were speaking Dutch, but their speech was generously sprinkled with English and some German. Finally, picking up no clues, Nancy decided to go to her cabin.

"Let's see, it's number one twenty-eight," she recalled. As she went down the steps, the *Winschoten* left the pier and started on her voyage to New York. When Nancy reached her stateroom, she opened the door and blinked in surprise. Bess and George were not there, but an attractive, fair-haired girl was seated on one of the four beds.

She rose immediately and smiled at Nancy. "Hello," she said. "I'm to be one of your roommates." She spoke with a slight accent. "My name is Nelda Detweiler. I'm the niece of the captain."

"I'm glad to meet you," Nancy said, shaking hands with the strange girl. "My two friends who

"What were you trying to do?" Bess asked.

are sharing this cabin with me should be here in a minute."

Nelda explained that she was from Johannesburg, South Africa, and that she had decided rather suddenly to attend college in the United States. "I was accepted immediately," she went on, "and I went to Rotterdam to see my uncle and his family. However, I almost had trouble getting on the ship, because it was booked out far in advance. The captain said there was an extra bed in this cabin, though, and I hope you and your friends don't mind my intruding."

Nelda was a beautiful girl and very charming. She had large brown eyes and a soft musical voice. Nancy liked her at once. However, she was still thinking of the message –EWARE NANCY DREW AND NE— and wondered if NE could refer to Nelda. Perhaps their new roommate was a spy?

"But she's so lovely," Nancy argued with herself. "I just can't believe there's anything dishonest about her." However, Nancy decided to watch Nelda carefully, at least for a while, and to warn Bess and George to be alert, too.

Aloud she assured the South African girl that the four companions would undoubtedly be very happy together.

"Oh, thank you," Nelda said and smiled. "I was afraid you might object to a stranger joining your group."

Soon Bess and George arrived. Nancy introduced them to Nelda Detweiler and explained how she happened to be rooming with them.

"How nice!" Bess exclaimed, and George smiled at the girl.

There was a knock on the door. George, who was nearest, opened it. A man walked in and introduced himself as Heinrich. "I'm your cabin steward," he said, and looked intensely at each girl. His eyes rested on Nelda for a longer time than on the others. Nancy wondered if there was any significance in this.

"Anything I can do for you, young ladies?" Heinrich asked.

"Not just now, thank you," Nancy replied.

The steward was forced to back into the hall because the luggage was arriving. Several suitcases were brought in by a porter. As the girls tried to stow them away, he set a brass-bound steamer trunk down in the middle of the floor. Across the front of it were two large initials: N.D.

Nancy tipped the porter, who left. Then she turned to Nelda. "This must be your trunk," she said. "I have a similar one, but this isn't mine."

Nelda turned to look at the piece of luggage. "No, I didn't bring a trunk."

Bess giggled. "There must be a third N.D. on board."

Nancy went to the door. "I'll try to catch the porter and tell him to take this one back," she said and hurried outside into the corridor.

It was crowded with baggage and passengers, and Nancy had to move slowly. The porter was not in sight, but just as Nancy was about to give up she heard loud talking from around the corner of a cross corridor.

"You took my trunk to the wrong cabin!" a man declared. "I saw you! And there were instructions on it to put it in the hold. Now please get it out of there and take it downstairs."

"Certainly, sir," another man replied. "Will you come with me and identify it, please?"

The first man mumbled something that Nancy could not understand, but she was sure the man was talking about the trunk in number one twenty-eight! She tried to make her way past suitcases and bundles to clear up the mistake, but by the time she reached the spot no one was there!

"That's strange," Nancy thought. "Maybe they weren't talking about the trunk in my cabin after all?"

She went back and found that more suitcases had arrived in the meantime. The mystery trunk, however, had not been picked up yet, nor had her own trunk been delivered.

"I almost found the owner," Nancy said to the others.

"What do you mean?" George asked.

Nancy told them about the conversation she had overheard, but, she explained, she had not found the man. She walked over to the trunk to examine it, thinking she might notify the owner. There were no stickers on it, nor any identification or handling instructions.

Nancy frowned. "This is really strange," she said. "I wonder if someone removed the tags, and if so, why?"

CHAPTER II

A Vain Search

NANCY and the other girls stared at the brass-bound trunk. They struggled to turn it over to see if there were stickers on the bottom of it, or any clue as to the owner, but they found nothing.

"This is very odd," Nelda said as they set the trunk upright again.

Bess remarked, "I heard someone say that pieces of baggage had been badly handled. Probably the tags on this were pulled off or knocked off accidentally."

"You could be right," Nancy said, but did not sound convinced. "Something tells me, however, that there is a mystery connected with this trunk. What I'm wondering right now is, could my trunk have been put in the hold instead of this one? After all, it has the same initials on it and looks identical."

"Why don't you go and find out?" George suggested.

"I will," Nancy replied, and stepped into the corridor again. She decided to go to the purser's office first. He might be able to tell her what to do about her lost luggage.

She hurried to the deck above and walked to the center of the ship. The assistant purser was on duty. According to a sign on the counter, his name was Mr. Rodman Havelock. He was about thirty years of age, sun-tanned, and good-looking. He smiled at Nancy. "May I help you?"

The girl introduced herself, then said, "There seems to have been a mix-up of trunks. One that does not belong to me came to my cabin, but it has my initials on it."

"Did you look at the number on the sticker?" Mr. Havelock asked.

"There are no stickers," Nancy replied. "That's just it. No identification whatsoever except the initials." She told the man about the conversation she had overheard in the corridor, then added, "Perhaps my trunk was taken into the hold instead of his?"

Mr. Havelock said he would look through the passenger list for someone else with the initials N.D. In a few moments he reported that the only two people aboard with those initials were Nancy Drew and her roommate Nelda Detweiler.

"But the trunk doesn't belong to Nelda either," Nancy said.

"Well, I'm afraid I can't help you on that score," Mr. Havelock said. "However, I will telephone the hold and ask if your trunk was delivered there by mistake." He dialed a number and spoke to someone in Dutch. Then he turned to Nancy again.

"I'm sorry, but they don't seem to have a record of it either."

Nancy caught her breath. A fearful feeling came over her. Perhaps through some mistake her trunk was not loaded aboard the *Winschoten* at all! "That would be dreadful," she thought. "No clothes to wear on the trip!"

The assistant purser spoke. "I'll do everything in my power to locate your trunk if it's on the ship, Miss Drew. There are mix-ups in the baggage sometimes. If yours went to the wrong cabin, the occupants will surely report it."

"I appreciate that very much, Mr. Havelock," Nancy replied.

The young man smiled. "How about calling me Rod? I'm more used to that."

"Okay—if you'll call me Nancy. And now I have another question."

"What's that?"

"Do you have a deaf person on board?" the girl inquired.

"I don't know," the assistant purser replied. "Why?"

Nancy decided not to divulge her suspicions until she knew Rod Havelock better, but she had not forgotten the message –EWARE NANCY DREW AND NE— in the finger language.

She told Rod that before the ship sailed she had seen a person on the pier talking in the finger alphabet to someone on the *Winschoten*. "I was just curious to know if only one of the people was deaf, or both," she explained.

Rod smiled. "I'll be glad to find out and let you know. The chief purser has a list of all persons aboard with any kind of physical disability. We try to give them special attention."

"Thanks," Nancy said, and went back to her cabin. At once the girls asked her what luck she had had.

"No luck with this trunk," she replied, "and none with mine, either. I see it hasn't arrived in the meantime."

Nelda said, "If you're worried about your clothes, I have tons with me. You look as though you're about my size and height. I'll be happy to lend you anything you want to borrow."

Nancy looked at her new-found friend and smiled. "That's wonderful of you, Nelda," she said. "Who knows? I might have to take your offer sooner than you think."

Nelda rose from her bed and opened one of her bags. From it she took a South African native's costume. It was made like a sheath, and gay red flowers and ferns had been embroidered on it. A wide sash of gold with a fringe on each end was intended to be the belt. Gold-colored sandals completed the outfit.

George giggled. "I can just see Nancy going

to the dining room for breakfast in this getup. It'll cause a stir!"

The others laughed. Nelda slipped the gown over Nancy's head, then adjusted the sash, which she wound around Nancy's slender body twice. Nelda's eyes were shining. "I understand there's a costume party on board one night," she said with enthusiasm. "Nancy, you must wear this!"

Nancy looked at herself in the mirror and smiled. "It is lovely, but I'm sure you brought it to wear yourself."

"Oh, I have something else I can put on," the girl replied. "Please use this outfit, Nancy."

Bess remarked, "Who in South Africa would wear a costume like this? All the pictures I've ever seen of the natives show dark-colored clothes."

Nelda laughed gaily. "This is a dress-up outfit," she said. "Nancy, see if you can wear the sandals. They're rather tight on me."

Nancy easily slipped her feet into the gold heelless sandals. "Aren't they pretty!" she exclaimed.

Bess said, "You look positively ravishing." She giggled. "You'd better watch your step. Don't captivate some young man on board and get your poor friend Ned Nickerson at home all worried!"

Nancy grinned. "Not a chance," she said. "Do you know who is the best-looking man I've seen on board so far?"

As the others shook their heads, she said, "It's the assistant purser, Rod Havelock."

Bess asked, "Well, there's no law on the high seas to prevent you from dancing with him, is there?"

"Oh, I'm sure there isn't," Nancy told her. "But sometimes officers are not allowed to mingle with passengers socially." She shrugged. "Anyway, he's probably married and has half-a-dozen children."

The teasing went on for several minutes, then they were interrupted. Someone knocked on the door. Before anyone answered, Nancy quickly slipped out of the costume and put her dress on. Then George went to the door.

She opened it and looked. "No one is out here!" she exclaimed, stepping into the corridor. Nobody was in sight!

"Somebody must be playing a joke on us," George said as she came back in and closed the door.

Nancy looked at her, then noticed a white envelope on the cabin floor just inside the door. "Wait a minute, George," she said. "Did you drop this?"

"No," George replied. She picked it up and turned it over. On the front was printed the name NELDA DETWEILER.

"It's for you," George said, and handed it to the South African girl.

"Oh, it must be from my uncle," Nelda said. "He's marvelous, you know. Wait until you meet him." She ripped the envelope open and stared at the card inside. Suddenly she turned deathly pale and fell down on the nearest bed.

"What's the matter?" Nancy inquired.

"Bad news?" George added kindly, and walked toward the girl.

Nelda held her hands over her face and began to weep. "I've been followed!" she cried out. "Oh, dear, I've been followed!"

CHAPTER III

The Jewel Thief

STARTLED by Nelda's outcry, Nancy, Bess, and George looked at one another.

"One thing is certain," Nancy thought. "She's terribly disturbed about something." She was forced, however, to recall her earlier suspicion that Nelda might be a spy. In that case the fact that she was followed would obviously upset her. But then, would she act like this?

Nancy's instinct told her to help the sobbing girl. She crossed the room, sat down beside her, and put her arms around Nelda.

"Is there anything we can do for you?" she asked.

"No, no," the distraught girl replied. "Thank you, thank you, but my problem is a big secret. I can't tell you."

Nancy did not know what to do. After all, Nelda was a stranger to her. She knew nothing of

17

her background. Her problem might indeed be one that she wanted to keep a secret, but then why did she admit that she had been followed?

Bess and George crossed the room also and stood in front of Nelda for a couple of seconds. Then George said, "You don't know, Nelda, but Nancy is an amateur detective. If your problem is some kind of a mystery, we're sure she can help you solve it, no matter how difficult it is."

Nelda looked up. Bess took a handkerchief and wiped the girl's tear-stained face. "Please stop crying," she begged.

Suddenly Nelda smiled. "Oh, you're so wonderful, all of you," she said. "My problem is a secret —a great secret—but I'm sure I can entrust it to you."

"Of course you can," George assured her.

"Promise?" Nelda asked.

When all nodded affirmatively, the girl looked relieved. She showed them the threatening note.

"As I told you before," she began her story, "I live in Johannesburg, South Africa. One day I was in a jewelry store to buy a birthday gift. A man stood at one of the counters, looking at diamond bracelets and rings on velvet pads."

She paused a moment, then went on, "He asked for something on display a little distance away. While the saleswoman was getting it, I saw him put two diamond bracelets and several rings in his pocket!"

"Oh, Nelda!" Bess cried out. "What did you do?"

"I was stunned. First I thought my eyes had played a trick on me, because I had watched the whole thing through a reflection in the glass of the display case. But when he hurried out of the store, I knew he had taken the jewelry. I yelled 'Stop, thief!' and sped after him to the street. But he was too quick for me and I lost sight of him."

"Oh, dear," George said. "Did you get the police?"

"No. I went back to the store and told the saleswoman. But she didn't believe me and insisted that I had taken the bracelets and rings myself! I tried to convince her I was not a thief, but just then a strange woman walked up. She said she had heard the argument, and when the manager came to see what was going on, she suggested that I be searched. 'Look in her pockets,' she said, and then walked away."

Bess interrupted, "And did they search you?"

Nelda nodded. "I told them I had nothing to hide. So they checked my pockets and to my utter astonishment, they pulled out a diamond bracelet!"

"How dreadful!" Bess exclaimed.

Nancy remarked, "What about the woman? Maybe she planted the bracelet in your pocket!"

"But why would she do that?" Nelda asked, puzzled.

"To divert suspicion from the man who stole the jewelry he had snatched when the saleswoman wasn't there," Nancy replied. "What did the thief look like?"

"He was of medium height, had black hair combed low over his forehead, a mustache, and a full, curly beard."

Nancy said, "No doubt that woman was an accomplice of the thief and was trying to throw suspicion on you."

Nelda looked at Nancy. "I can see why you're a detective. I'll bet that is exactly what happened."

"Please go on with your story," Bess urged.

Nelda said that her parents and a lawyer had helped her convince proprietors of the store that she was not a thief, and they had pressed no charges against her. "We all thought the matter would end there," the girl explained, "but that was not the case."

"What happened then?" George asked.

"I received a threatening letter. It was not signed, but the writer said I should turn over all the precious jewelry in my family or I would be harmed."

"Nelda, that was dreadful!" Bess exclaimed. "What did you do?"

"My father reported the matter to the police, and they promised to investigate. But we kept getting threats in the mail and over the telephone, and my dad decided it would be best if I left the country for a while. So I applied to an American college and was accepted. I left Johannesburg secretly and flew to Rotterdam, where I stayed with my uncle, the captain of this ship."

Nelda paused, then smiled wanly. "I've told you the rest already. Of course I had no idea that you would become involved in this mystery."

"I'm glad to be," Nancy said, "and not only I, but Bess and George, too. They're good amateur detectives also. We'll help you."

"Oh, how lucky I am to have found such great new friends!" Nelda said.

Bess looked toward Nancy. "Where do you think we should begin?"

The girl replied, "Either the thief Nelda saw in Johannesburg or one of his confederates is obviously on board this ship. Nelda, do you think you could identify the man you watched in the jewelry shop?"

"I'm sure I could," Nelda replied.

"Then let's hunt for him," Nancy suggested. "We'll walk every deck and lounge."

Bess reminded her friends that it was almost time for dinner. They were to sit at the captain's table and realized they should not be late. As it was the first night, dress was casual and Nancy did not have to worry about changing her clothes.

The girls went to the dining room, where they met Captain Detweiler, a tall, burly man whom they liked immediately.

After dinner, they spent the rest of the evening looking intently at every man they saw on their trek over the entire ship. At no time did Nelda indicate that she recognized anyone. The girls realized that there was no one who would even remotely fit the description Nelda had given them.

Finally, the foursome became weary of searching. Bess giggled and said:

> We saw men tall and short,
> Men of every size,
> Some were dark, some were blond,
> But none was our prize!

George laughed. "But you'll get the prize for best cornball poet of the year!"

Nancy sighed. "If that thief is on board, he must have remained in his cabin. On the other hand, there may be a ring of jewel thieves. I've heard that there are rings in which some members steal, others transport and even smuggle. A third group sells the stolen property. Your bearded man, Nelda, may still be in Johannesburg."

Nelda nodded. "Then we have no idea whom we're looking for and what clue we should follow."

"Right." Nancy was tempted to tell Nelda about the warning she had observed being given with the finger alphabet. She was inclined to think that the unfinished word starting with NE in the message stood for Nelda, but decided not to say anything yet. The girl from Johannesburg had enough problems.

Bess continued her doggerel.

> We'd better watch our step,
> Especially Nelda, dear,
> But never, never fear,
> We'll catch that bad man yet!

The other girls laughed, but all had to admit that they had not a single lead to help them to do just that.

Nelda said, "My uncle invited us up to his quarters. Let's go and tell him everything that has happened."

The others agreed, and soon they were seated in the captain's comfortable living room, telling him about the threatening note Nelda had received and their vain search for the man who had written it.

Captain Detweiler looked grave. "This is a very serious matter," he said.

Nancy now brought him up-to-date on the story of her missing trunk and the strange one that had been delivered to the girls' cabin.

The captain frowned. "You say there's no identification of any kind on this mystery trunk? In that case I feel I have a right to open it and find out if there are any clues to the owner."

"Unless we can find the man I overheard in the corridor," Nancy put in. "He might own the trunk."

The captain nodded. "First I'll talk to all the stewards and porters and see if I can find out who the man is. If I'm not successful and if he does not come forward on his own, I'll send Lou, the locksmith, to your cabin tomorrow to open the trunk. I might not be able to be there myself, but"—he smiled at Nancy—"since you are a detective, you'll find any identification that might be inside."

Nancy smiled back. "I'm sure I will. But do you have any idea where my own trunk could be? Mr. Havelock has already called the hold, but they have no record of it."

"When I talk to the porters, I'll pursue this also. Perhaps someone put it in the wrong cabin."

"Thank you very much," Nancy said. "And now I think we should leave. Good night."

Bess and George said good night also, and Nelda kissed her uncle.

"Take care, all of you," he said to them.

George suggested that before going to their cabin, they should stroll on the promenade deck. "We might even find the man we're looking for," she added.

The others agreed and they set off. They met a group of girls about their own age and introduced themselves. The newcomers were chatting about their departure and the facilities on the ocean liner.

"They have a lovely outdoor pool here," a tall brunette named Sara Jane Ramsey said. "And there's another one indoors, way at the bottom of the ship."

"And there are Ping-Pong tables and shuffle-board," another girl reported. "We'll have a great time during our trip."

One of the girls admired Nancy's light-blue summer dress.

"I'm glad you like it," Nancy replied and laughed. "You might see me in it for the rest of the voyage!" She told the girls that she had not received her trunk, but did not mention the mystery trunk that had been sent to her cabin by mistake.

The girls immediately offered to lend her clothes, but Nancy thanked them and said she would have enough from her friends. Then they said good-by to the group and went on.

They were halfway around the deck when Bess suddenly cried out, "Look! Look!"

A bright object was descending from the sky at lightning speed.

"It must be a meteor!" Nelda said, excited.

"And it's going to land on this ship!" George exclaimed. "We'll all be killed!"

CHAPTER IV

Inquisitive Locksmith

NOT only the four girls, but all the passengers who saw the object coming, froze in fear! Then, for several seconds, there was near panic on board the *Winschoten*. Women screamed. Men shouted warnings. Children cried. But the first fright was over quickly. The whizzing meteor crashed into the ocean not far from the ship.

Within seconds, its tremendous splash caused a tidal wave that nearly swamped the *Winschoten*. The ship dipped and rose on the mighty swell that followed.

Nancy and her friends tried to hold on to the railing but found it impossible. Some unseen force seemed to yank their hands away. As they sprawled on the deck, they narrowly missed being trampled by other passengers who also had lost their footing.

Chairs were sliding about helter-skelter. Some held people; others were empty. Cries of pain rang out. Officers yelled orders over loudspeakers in vain. Passengers tried to stand, but were unable to.

The *Winschoten* rose and dipped, then swung from side to side as if it were a giant rocking cradle. Little by little quiet was restored to the sea. The great ocean liner stabilized and the upheaval ceased.

Nancy, Bess, Nelda, and George called out to one another and were glad that none of them had been injured. Many passengers had not fared so well. Some struggled to their feet and hobbled off to their cabins. Others had to be taken to the infirmary.

Nancy and her friends helped wherever they could. They pulled deck chairs off people who were pinned beneath them, and comforted frightened children.

Suddenly over the loudspeaker came a strong voice. "This is your captain speaking. I wish to report that our ship has not been damaged in any way and that we are proceeding on our regular course. Passengers needing medical attention please come to the infirmary or the lounge nearest you. If you are unable to get there yourself, please ask others to help you."

An elderly woman near the girls was crying.

She said her back had been injured. "I can't move," she sobbed. "Please get a doctor! Oh, oh, I can't stand it!"

Someone brought a stretcher, and gently Nancy and her friends lifted the woman onto it. As carefully as possible the girls carried the frail, sobbing passenger downstairs to the infirmary.

Many people were already there, waiting to see one of the two doctors. Nurses, smiling encouragingly, were hurrying about as more and more passengers were coming in or being carried to an inner room, where the most seriously injured were being treated.

Nancy thought it best that she and her friends leave as quickly as possible to make room for the patients. Two nurses relieved them of their burden; then the girls hurried upstairs and went directly to their cabin. All were exhausted from the shock and dropped onto their beds.

"What a dreadful experience we have been through!" Nelda said. "That meteor was close."

The others nodded, and Bess said, "Just think how many fish and plants were killed or badly shocked by it!"

Nancy was thoughtful. She admitted she had been frightened, but finally changed the subject and announced she was going to undress and get under the covers.

"Who'll lend me a nightie?" she asked, looking around.

George grinned. "I have just the thing for you. I'm going to wear it at the costume party, but you're welcome to sleep in it."

From her suitcase, she brought out a long, white flannel grandmother nightgown with a matching cap. The girls giggled.

"Before I use it," George said, "I'm going to sew fake mice all over it." She reached into her suitcase again. "Here are the candleholder and candle I'm going to carry."

"You'll certainly win a prize," Nelda predicted. "That is very funny. But you ought to have a long braid hanging down your back."

"And here it is!" George held up a hairpiece. "Nancy, try on the outfit, will you?"

The light banter helped the girls relax after their harrowing experience, and Nancy was glad to go along with it. Quickly she undressed and slipped into the old-fashioned nightie. She adjusted the cap and the braid, then looked at herself in the mirror.

"Do I look like my great-great-great-great grandmother?" she asked, trying to make her voice sound old and feeble.

The girls laughed. "It's perfect," George said.

Nancy made a face, then took off the cap. "George, I don't want to get it wrinkled by wearing it to bed. Will someone please lend me another nightgown?"

Bess obliged her by handing her a pale-blue silk

nightie, and that was what Nancy wore. She grinned. "This doesn't look bad on me either," she said. "Maybe I'll like it so well I won't give it back to you!"

Bess pretended to take the remark seriously. "Hey, I didn't know you were a thief!"

Before each girl went to sleep, she said a prayer of thanks for being unhurt at a time when there might have been a great catastrophe.

Directly after breakfast the next morning, Lou, the locksmith, came to the girls' cabin. He was a small, talkative Dutchman who said he lived in England. He and his father had made a study of locks from very early times, not only in historic England, but all over the world.

"Do you know what the first lock was?" he asked the girls.

When they said no, he explained that it was just two pieces of wood nailed upright beyond the edges of a door. Then a long bar was slipped through them to hold the door shut.

"And to keep intruders out," George added.

Lou crossed the room and looked at the mysterious brass-bound trunk. He opened a little satchel he carried with him and took out a large metal ring to which were attached many keys.

"Is this the piece you can't open?" he asked.

"Yes," Nancy replied.

"Lost the key?"

She did not answer, and he did not pursue his

question. Instead, he tried the keys one by one in the lock, but none of them would fit. Finally he put them back into his bag.

"Guess I'll have to try something more intricate," he said. "This lock has hidden tumblers. That's harder than anything else to open. It's the best kind of lock, though, because it can only be opened with a special key. Leavers are used mostly in standard or stock keys."

When Lou was not speaking aloud, he was mumbling to himself either in Dutch or in English. Nancy caught phrases like *pin tumbler, too much graphite, bent key, cam screws,* and wondered what he was thinking. All the girls figured that in any case, opening the mystery trunk was not an easy job.

"Hm!" Lou said at last. "You must have something valuable in here, Miss Drew, to lock it up this way!"

The girls looked at one another, but made no comment. The locksmith did not seem to notice their lack of response. After he had tried several more keys, Lou said, "I guess I'll just have to remove the cylinder."

Using a tiny screw driver to take out the set screw, he released the cylinder. In a few moments he found the secret of the combination, and filed a new key. Then he returned the cylinder to its plate and handed the key to Nancy. "Try this," he said.

She did. "Oh, it fits perfectly!" she said, pleased. She had no trouble locking and unlocking the mystery trunk.

Lou rose and put his tools away. Again he spoke to Nancy. "You'd better not lose this key," he told her. Then he stared in amazement at the trunk. Nelda had opened it, and revealed part of its contents.

"Well, well!" Lou exclaimed. "Men's clothes!" He looked at Nancy quizzically. "Are you masquerading or perhaps you are part of a traveling theater group?" he asked her pointedly.

Bess giggled, but the other two girls frowned. Nancy merely smiled. "Guess again," she said.

Lou was not sure what she meant by this, but she gave him no time for other questions. Instead, she took his arm, escorted him to the door, and opened it.

"Thank you very much," she said, handing him several *guilders* for his work. "I'll let you know if I have any more trouble." Then she almost pushed him into the corridor, shut the door behind him, and locked it.

The other girls were laughing, but finally became quiet. "So N.D. is a man!" George remarked.

"That doesn't surprise me," Nancy said. "I still think it's that fellow I overheard in the corridor."

At this moment there was a knock on the door.

George walked over and opened it. Heinrich, their cabin steward, stood there.

"Lou, the locksmith, thought maybe you needed some help," he said and stepped inside.

"I don't think so," George said. "But thanks for the offer." She tried to usher him out, but he stood still and stared at the open trunk.

"Your boyfriend's clothes?" he said to Nancy, smirking.

"No," George said and escorted him into the corridor. She shut the door, locked it, and walked back to the trunk.

"Nancy, I'm afraid your reputation will be ruined forever. No doubt Heinrich will spread the word around that you have your boyfriend stashed away under your bed!"

"I'll set them straight," Nancy replied with a chuckle. "I'll tell them he's yours, not mine!"

After the teasing subsided, George asked, "What do you suggest we do next with this?"

Nancy replied, "I think we should invite the captain to come down here and investigate this trunk with us. Nelda, would you please call him? If he isn't in his quarters, try other locations."

Nelda picked up the phone and after several attempts reached her uncle. She told him what the trunk contained and that they were about to empty it.

"I'll be right down," he said.

Not only Captain Detweiler but the girls were amazed at what he pulled out of the mystery trunk. On top were good-looking suits, but underneath was an assortment of old, worn outfits, paint-spotted overalls, and a battered black felt hat.

"This seems like a working man's trunk on the bottom and an executive's on top," Bess remarked.

The captain continued to pull articles out. He held up a gray and a red wig.

"Disguises!" George exclaimed. "Assuming that the man doesn't have a wig in his own color, he could either be a blond or a brunette."

"Or he could be bald," Bess added.

Captain Detweiler turned to Nancy. "What is your opinion?"

"I believe the owner of this trunk wears disguises for some reason, perhaps one that isn't entirely honest. By the way, captain, did you have a chance to ask the porters about the man I overheard in the corridor?"

"Yes. One of them remembered the incident, but said the fellow left after complaining that his trunk had been delivered to the wrong cabin, and hasn't said anything since then."

"Does the porter know who it was?"

"No. He said he didn't pay much attention because he was so busy distributing the luggage."

"That's strange," Nancy said. "The fact that

the passenger didn't follow up on his trunk seems to indicate that he felt uneasy about it. And if this is it, he might have been afraid someone would open it and find all these disguises!"

"Sounds logical," the captain admitted.

The searchers were interrupted by a knock on the door. Quickly they restored the contents of the trunk and pulled down the lid. Then Nancy went to admit the caller.

Heinrich stood there again, but did not attempt to enter. He merely said, "I have a message for you, Miss Drew. Mr. Havelock wants to see you at once at the purser's desk!"

CHAPTER V

Crashing Trunks

"THANK you," Nancy said to the steward. "I'll go up in a few minutes." He left and she rejoined her friends.

"I wonder why the purser's office didn't phone instead of giving the message to Heinrich," she thought to herself. "This may be a hoax!"

Just then the telephone rang. It was for Captain Detweiler. A ship's officer was calling to tell him that he was needed on the bridge at once.

After saying he would be there directly, the captain hung up and smiled at the girls. "I'll leave this mystery in your hands," he said. "And I'm sure you'll solve it."

"It has us puzzled," Nancy admitted. "But we'll do our best."

The captain patted the young sleuth on the shoulder as he left, then Nancy turned to the girls. "You heard Heinrich's message, didn't you? I'm supposed to go up to the purser."

Her three friends wanted to accompany her, but Nancy had another idea. "This might be a ruse to get us all out of the cabin," she said. "Then someone could come in and either take the mystery trunk or unpack it and take away the contents."

Nelda nodded. "I'll stay here," she offered. "You go ahead."

Bess said that she, too, would stay. "If more than one person should come in and make a scene, two of us might be able to get them out of here better than one."

"Okay," Nancy said.

The trunk was locked and shoved under her bed. Only a little of the brass trimming showed. Nancy looked around for a place to hide the new key to it. Finally she decided. "I'll put it in the secret pocket inside my cosmetic bag."

She and George went to the purser's office. Mr. Rodman Havelock was there and said that he, indeed, had sent the message by Heinrich. "Your line was busy when I tried to call, so I asked the steward to tell you."

Nancy and George were relieved. The message had not been a ruse after all!

"I think I have good news for you," Rod went on. "After the meteor came down and the ship was tilting and listing, many pieces of luggage in the hold were dislodged. While straightening the place up, the man in charge spotted a brass-bound trunk marked N.D. under a heap of other baggage. It must be yours."

"Wonderful!" Nancy exclaimed. "How soon can it be sent to my cabin?"

The assistant purser suggested that first she go to the hold and identify the trunk to be absolutely sure it was hers.

"We don't want any more mix-ups," he added.

Rod wrote out a slip to the man in charge of the hold, saying Nancy and George had permission to enter and look at the trunk. Then he gave them directions.

"Thank you very much," Nancy said, and the two girls hurried off.

They found the door leading down steep iron steps to the boiler room. The place fascinated them, not only because of the huge fire pits, but also because of the pipes and myriads of electrical wires leading to every part of the ship.

Nancy and George had to walk carefully because of the small puddles of oil here and there, which had dripped from the machinery.

George grinned. "We'd be a mess if we fell here," she commented.

The girls were intrigued by the gigantic pipes running along either side of the ship, which held fresh drinking water.

Finally they came to the hold. The door was locked, so they pushed a button, which rang a bell inside.

A crewman opened it. Nancy showed him the permission slip and he allowed the girls to enter. The heavy door locked behind them with a great thud. The man, on whose overalls was stitched the name Pieter, said something to them in Dutch, but when Nancy indicated she could not speak his language, he pointed and led the way to where the trunk was stored.

At this very moment, the ship lurched. Pieter, Nancy, and George lost their balance. All three of them fell to the wooden floor. Baggage and boxes tumbled about, pinning them down. At the same time all the lights in the hold went out.

The crewman cried out in pain. George was silent. Nancy could not move, but called out, "George, are you all right?"

There was no reply, not even a muffled answer to her frantic question. Instead, speaking with a Dutch inflection, Pieter said, "Ring gong by door!"

In the blackness Nancy pushed away an enormous box and struggled to her feet. Then she tried to find her way to where she thought the door was. The girl detective kept bumping into various kinds of baggage and pushing them aside. It was hard going, but she urged herself on. Obviously Pieter was in no condition to move.

Once she concluded she had gone in a circle and started over again.

"Hurry!" Pieter cried out.

"I'm trying!" Nancy replied.

Finally she could feel the outline of the great steel door and moved her fingers alongside it. At last they discovered a round object, which she assumed was a bell. Nancy pushed it hard. A loud gong began to ring in the corridor outside.

Within minutes there was a knock on the door. "What's the matter?" boomed a man's deep voice. "Are you having trouble in there?"

Nancy put her face against the doorjamb and shouted, "We're locked in and two people are hurt. Please let us out!"

Someone began to manipulate the lock on the other side and presently the big door swung open. A powerful flashlight was beamed into Nancy's blinking eyes. "What happened?" asked the ship's officer who stood there. She had never seen him before, but he gave his name as Harper.

"There was this big lurch," Nancy said, "and the lights went out in the hold. My friend and I were in here with Pieter to look for my trunk, when we were all thrown down. I think Pieter is hurt, and my friend may be, too!"

Mr. Harper beamed his flashlight all around. In a moment it picked up Pieter's prostrate form. He was lying face down with a heavy crate on top of him, and he was moaning in pain.

The ship gave a tremendous lurch.

The officer hurried over to the stricken figure. "Come on," he said, "help me get this crate off him!"

With great effort he and Nancy lifted the crate from the man and helped him stand up. He was able to walk around and move his arms, but said his head hurt.

Mr. Harper told him to take several deep breaths, and Pieter did so without showing any discomfort. Apparently he had not injured his ribs.

"You're lucky nothing seems to be broken," the officer said to him.

Nancy spoke. "Please come and help me find my friend. She must be unconscious!"

All three made their way to George's side. Her eyes were closed and she did not move, but there was no luggage lying on her.

"She might have hit her head," Mr. Harper said. "We must have her taken to the infirmary. She needs attention right away."

While Nancy stayed with George, Mr. Harper stepped into the corridor and used a wall telephone. He called the infirmary and suggested that a doctor come at once and that orderlies bring a stretcher to take a patient upstairs.

Nancy had been rubbing George's wrists and the back of her neck, trying to restore her to consciousness. But there was no response from her friend.

"Oh, George, please wake up!" Nancy pleaded and rubbed harder. George did not stir.

An icy fear crept up Nancy's spine and her heart began to beat wildly. Suppose George's injuries had been fatal!

CHAPTER VI

The Secret Plan

SUDDENLY the excitement, exertion, and worry swept over Nancy. Objects in the hold around her began to waver and grow dim. Her head spun, then everything was black!

When Nancy woke up, she felt as if she had been asleep a long time. She realized she was lying on a table in the examining room. A nurse was standing beside her, smiling.

"You must have fainted," she said kindly. "Here, drink this!" The young woman handed Nancy a paper cup containing a hot liquid. "I'm sure it'll make you feel better."

The girl sat up and sipped the refreshing stimulant. She wondered what the concoction was. It tasted like a combination of tea, cinnamon, sugar, and something very bitter. In seconds Nancy felt much better, and gradually the events of the past half hour came back to her. She remembered George and the accident in the ship's hold. "My friend," she said to the nurse. "What happened to her?" The fear for George returned and showed in Nancy's tense voice.

"She's all right," the nurse said.

"Is she awake? Can I talk to her?"

"I'll find out for you. Meanwhile, I suggest you take it easy."

"All right," Nancy said.

When the nurse had left the room, she slid off the table and went to sit in a comfortable leather chair. For a few minutes she felt drowsy again, but presently she was wide awake and sat up straight.

The nurse reappeared and said, "You may come with me and see your friend now."

"Oh, thanks!" Nancy felt as if a great weight had been lifted from her shoulders. She followed the nurse into a tiny pleasant room. George was lying in the only bed.

"Oh, I'm so happy to see you awake!" Nancy exclaimed, kissing her. "What does the doctor say?"

Before George could answer, a physician appeared and introduced himself as Dr. Karl. He answered the question himself.

"Your friend George is lucky not to have been injured worse. She did get a good bump on the head. No permanent damage has been done, though. She'll have to remain here for twenty-four hours for observation."

George smiled. "I'm terribly sorry, Nancy. I guess I won't be able to help you for a while."

"Don't worry about that," Nancy said. "Right now you just get better."

The young detective thought perhaps Bess and Nelda would like to come for a short visit, so she picked up George's bedside telephone and dialed one twenty-eight. There was no reply at first, but finally Bess answered.

"Oh, Nancy," she said, "something terrible has happened. Please come right back to the cabin and hurry!"

"What's the matter?" Nancy asked.

"Two men came in here to rob us!" Bess cried out.

"Okay, I'll be right there," Nancy said and hung up. She decided not to tell George what Bess had said and waved good-by. "I'll be back soon," she told the girl. "Right now I'll have to go and find out about my trunk. We never did finish our job."

When Nancy walked into one twenty-eight she found Nelda and Bess seated on one of the beds. Both girls were shaking like leaves.

"What happened?" Nancy asked.

"Oh, it was awful, just awful!" Bess replied. "Heinrich brought two strange men here. He said they were plumbers and had come to fix our shower. After the steward was gone, I told the men nothing was wrong with our shower. They looked anyway then returned and said yes, it was okay."

"That's when the trouble started," Nelda put in. They came back into our room and one of them saw the brass-bound trunk!"

"He yanked it out from under the bed," Bess continued. "I asked him why he was doing that, and he told me he recognized it. The trunk was supposed to be in the hold."

Nelda added, "But we told them they couldn't have it. Then one of them said it belonged to a friend of his and they were going to take it whether we liked it or not."

"But they didn't," Nancy remarked.

Nelda smiled. "Because we wouldn't let them!"

"Don't think they didn't try," Bess added. "They pushed us out of the way and tried to grab it. When they did that, we both screamed. They got scared, I guess, and ran out of the cabin."

"Did anyone else hear you?" Nancy asked.

"Yes. Within seconds Heinrich, another steward, and two or three passengers arrived. They did their best to calm us."

"I'm sure," Nancy said, "that those men weren't ship's plumbers. They suspected or were told that an unmarked trunk with the initials N. D. on it was in here and decided to have a look."

"More than that," Bess said, "they decided to steal it!"

Nelda told Nancy that she had asked the two strangers for the name of their friend who allegedly owned the trunk, and one of them had answered in an ugly tone that it was none of her business.

Nancy asked what the two intruders looked like.

"They both had blondish beards and mustaches," Nelda said.

Nancy thought about the disguises in the trunk. The owner could have more of the same in a suitcase in his cabin. She doubted that the beards were real! But she did not say anything and tried to calm the nervous girls.

Bess said, "Probably we've not seen the last of those two villains. Nancy, they threatened that if we said anything about their being here and trying to take the trunk, we'd be harmed!"

Nelda added, "And they insisted that they'd be back. They want that trunk!"

"This is serious," Nancy stated. "I think I'll call Rod Havelock. He goes off duty just about this time. Maybe he'll come up here and give us some advice as to what we should do about this."

She phoned the purser's office and found that the assistant was indeed about to leave. "I'll see you in a few minutes," he promised.

While waiting for him, Nancy told Bess and Nelda about the accident in the hold, and that George was in the infirmary.

Bess, already distraught, burst into tears. "Oh, my poor cousin! Nancy, tell me exactly what happened and how she is!"

Nancy reported that the doctor had said George would be all right, but she must remain in bed for twenty-four hours.

"That isn't so bad," Bess said finally. "I'm glad she was not seriously hurt."

A few minutes of silence followed, then Nelda said, "Obviously those two men weren't plumbers. Do you think they might have been passengers in disguise, Nancy?"

"I do. But I'd like to check with the maintenance crew, anyway, just to make sure. Could you two identify the men?"

Both Bess and Nelda were sure they could, provided the men's beards were real.

There was a tap on the door. Bess and Nelda jumped, but Nancy told them she was sure it was Rod Havelock. She opened the door and the assistant purser stepped inside. He greeted the girls pleasantly. "What's your problem?" he asked. "I'll be glad to help if I can."

When he heard about the accident in the hold and the episode in the cabin, his expression became grave.

"Those two intruders must have watched Nancy and George leave, and they knew only Nelda and Bess were in the cabin," he reasoned. "And they thought they could handle the two of you. What did they look like?"

When he heard about the beards, he shook his head. "No one in the maintenance crew fits that description as far as I know. But I'll make some inquiries and see if those so-called plumbers are part of the crew elsewhere."

"Thank you," Nancy said. "Now, we have something to show you."

She got the key to the mystery trunk and swung open the lid. She held up the worn workman's clothes and the wigs.

Havelock whistled. "Obviously the owner of this trunk is an artist in disguises," he said. "Maybe he's a criminal and is afraid to claim his property for that reason."

He stared off into space a couple of seconds, then added, "In thinking this over, I believe the trunk should not be taken to the hold."

"You mean we should keep it here?" Nelda asked.

"If we do, we'll get into trouble!" Bess added.

Havelock shook his head. "I have an idea. The adjoining cabin is vacant. It had been booked, but the people who were supposed to occupy it missed the ship. I'll get you keys for it."

He pointed to a connecting door in the girls' room. "You see, the two open into each other, and each has a connecting door that can be opened only from the inside. I'll unlock both and leave the keys with you."

"And we'll hide the trunk in the other cabin?" Bess asked.

"Yes. We can carry it quietly from here to there and hide it in the wardrobe. Heinrich won't go in since no one is staying in number one thirty."

"That's a great idea," said Nancy. "Then we can investigate the trunk further. I really can't believe that someone would want these clothes so badly that he would threaten people. Perhaps something much more valuable is hidden in the trunk!"

Havelock nodded. "You may have a point there. By the way, did you find your own trunk in the hold?"

"I caught a glimpse of it," Nancy replied, "just before the ship gave a great roll and knocked some of the cargo over. But I think I could locate it."

"What happened to Pieter?" Rod Havelock asked.

"He was taken to the infirmary along with George, who hit her head. Perhaps he's still being treated. I don't know how serious his injury is."

"I'll find out," the assistant purser offered. He picked up the telephone and called the infirmary. The nurse told him that Pieter was being kept there until the following afternoon, but that he was not seriously hurt.

Havelock hung up and turned to Nancy. "Pieter will be all right. Now suppose we get your trunk up here and put it where the other one is. If the intruders should come again, you can let them have a closer look and they'll realize it's not what they want."

"Good idea," Nancy said. "But suppose they see us bring it up?"

"We'll have to do it at night when everyone is in bed. How about two-thirty A.M.? By that time the entertainment will be over and most people will have retired. I doubt that we would meet anybody then."

"Great!" Nancy was excited at the prospect of the adventure, and also about having her own clothes.

At bedtime, when the other girls changed into their nighties and robes, Nancy put on a pair of blue jeans and a sweater of George's. The three girls tried to sleep but it was hopeless. Finally they began to whisper.

"How do you suppose those two men knew the mystery trunk was in our cabin?" Bess asked.

"Perhaps they saw the porter carry it in," Nancy replied. "Or they might have found out it was not in the hold and questioned all the stewards until they located it."

Nelda said, "I wonder if Heinrich is entirely innocent or if he's somehow mixed up in the mystery. He knew there was nothing wrong with our shower, and since he works on the ship, wouldn't he know the plumbers?"

Nancy shrugged. "Not necessarily. Sometimes

they hire people just before a trip. As for the shower, they could have told him there was a leak somewhere else, which could have been caused by our pipes."

"I think he's honest," Bess said. "Merely inquisitive." She looked at her watch. "Nancy, it's almost two-thirty. You'd better get ready to go."

Just then there was a tap on the door. As Nancy walked toward it, Bess warned. "Watch out. It may not be Mr. Havelock after all!"

CHAPTER VII

Nelda Is Missing

NANCY opened the corridor door an inch and looked out before admitting the caller. She was pleased to see Rod Havelock standing there. "Come in," she said.

The assistant purser stepped inside, closed the door, and took a ring of keys from his pocket. He walked over and greeted the other girls. "I have all the keys you'll need for the adjoining cabin," he said. "I suggest that you hide them until Nancy and I get back from our little excursion."

Rod grinned and explained what each key was for. "The one with the blue mark will open the connecting door from this cabin to one thirty. Beyond it you'll find another door, which opens into the other cabin, but you can't unlock it from this side."

"You mean we'll have to enter cabin one thirty from the corridor?" Bess asked.

"That's right. With the yellow key. And this red one opens the connecting door from one thirty to one twenty-eight. I suggest that you bolt the corridor door from the inside and leave the bolt in place. Then unlock the connecting door from one thirty and leave it open for the rest of the trip so you can go next door without stepping into the hallway. Is that clear?"

"It's as clear as mud." Bess giggled.

Rod went on, "I think all of us should know where you are going to hide the keys. Does anyone have an idea?"

The girls looked around and finally Nelda pointed out that there was a tiny drawer on the back wall of their wardrobe.

"That's a good suggestion," Rod Havelock agreed. "Here, take them."

He handed the keys to Nelda, who immediately put them in the hiding place. Then he said to Nancy, "Let's go!" He peered into the corridor and announced that no one was in sight. "Come on!"

Nancy slipped the key to one twenty-eight into her pocket, then the two set off. They did not rush but walked on tiptoe to avoid calling attention to themselves.

They reached the iron stairway to the boiler room and descended. The men on duty nodded to Havelock but did not ask any questions as the couple headed for the hold. Rod unlocked the heavy steel door, then he switched on the overhead lights.

"I'm glad the lights were fixed," Nancy said, crossing the heavy plank floorway. She led the way toward the area where she had seen the trunk she thought might be hers. It was still there, but crewmen had evidently piled up some of the baggage that had fallen down.

"That's my trunk, all right," the girl stated. For the first time she noticed that a net had been stretched across this part of the hold to keep the baggage in place. But the upheaval caused by the meteor had torn it to shreds.

Rod said, "I think we can get it out of there easily enough." He smiled. "You look like a strong girl."

As Nancy examined the baggage around her own piece, she suddenly found herself staring into the face of a rat. It seemed to be wedged tightly between her trunk and a heavy box.

"Oh!" She let out a stifled scream.

"What's the matter?" Rod Havelock asked anxiously.

Nancy explained and the assistant purser came to look at the little animal himself.

"We'll just let him loose," he said. "The rat will be more scared of us than we are of him. He'll run off in a hurry."

Reaching up, he yanked aside the trunk next to Nancy's. But the menacing rat did not scoot away as predicted!

Suddenly Nancy began to laugh. "Rod, he's dead!"

Havelock laughed too. "The joke's on us, all right," he remarked.

He lifted the rodent by the tail and flung it off to one side. Then he and Nancy set to work to loosen her trunk. By manipulating it from side to side, they were finally able to pull it forward.

"We'd better be careful of the box on top of it," Nancy said. "We don't want to break anything."

Gently the box was shoved backward so it would not fall. Then Rod and Nancy took hold of the leather handle on each side of her trunk and eased it out. It was tedious work, but finally it was released.

After they had carried the trunk to the door and set it down, the assistant purser said, "My, this is heavy! Nancy Drew, are you sure there isn't part of a gold mine from South Africa in there?"

The girl laughed. "No, but I bought a lot of gifts and souvenirs."

She assured her companion that she was strong enough to carry the trunk with his help. He clicked off the light and locked the hold. Then he opened the door that led into the engine room and called softly to one of the men, "Will you help me get this up the stairs, please?"

"*Ja, ja,*" a burly engineer replied, and came over.

Nancy was glad he asked no questions. The two

men lugged the trunk up to the deck above, then the engineer returned to his post.

Nancy picked up one end of the trunk, and again she and Rod tiptoed along corridors until they came to cabin one twenty-eight.

Nancy unlocked the door and the two carried the brass-bound piece inside and set it down. The lights were on, and Bess was seated on the side of her bed.

"We got it!" Nancy said jubilantly.

Bess showed no enthusiasm and made no comment. Instead she cried out, "I'm dreadfully worried. Nelda has disappeared!"

"What!" Nancy exclaimed in disbelief. "Where? When? How?"

"I don't know," Bess replied miserably. "I had fallen asleep but heard a slight noise and woke up. I thought it was you. When I turned on the light and looked around, I discovered that Nelda was not here."

"Where do you suppose she went?" Rod Havelock asked.

Nancy and Bess had no idea.

The assistant purser added practically, "Wherever she's gone, I'm sure she'll be back." Then he said in a whisper, "I suggest that we move the mystery trunk into the cabin next door as soon as possible, and put yours under your bed, Nancy, before you have any more inquisitive visitors coming here to try to take it away from you."

Nancy opened the girls' wardrobe and pulled out the little drawer in back of it. The keys were gone!

Bess cried out, "Someone has been here and taken Nelda away and stolen the keys! And it's all my fault for not staying awake!"

Nancy was alarmed. She said, "I don't understand, though. If that's the case, why didn't the intruder take the mystery trunk with him?"

There was complete silence. Suddenly Nancy had an idea. She walked toward the door and tried the knob. The door was not locked, and neither was the one on the other side!

Quickly Nancy stepped into cabin one thirty. The light was on. As she looked around, Bess and Rod walked in. All of them stared at a heap on the bed covered with a blanket. Could it be Nelda?

Bess cried out, "M-maybe she's d-dead! Oh, I can't stand it!"

Nancy, too, was fearful that the people who had threatened Nelda had really carried out some horrible scheme. While Bess was sobbing and still blaming herself, Nancy walked over to the bed and pulled off the blanket. Nelda lay there. She did not move!

"She's asleep!" Rod said.

"Are you sure?" Bess sobbed.

Nelda was awakened by the voices. She looked around wildly. "Help! Help!" she exclaimed.

Nancy touched the girl gently. "Nelda, wake up, please!" she said.

"No! No! I'm awake," Nelda insisted. "But some awful man who knew about my trouble back home phoned me after you left the room. Bess was asleep and didn't hear it. He said he would throw me overboard if I ever mentioned the Johannesburg incident to anyone!"

"Oh, how awful!" Bess wailed.

Nelda went on, "I didn't know what to do. My first thought was to run. Then I remembered this vacant cabin and decided to come here. I took the keys out of the little drawer and opened all the doors. But I locked the corridor door of cabin one thirty and bolted it from the inside."

There was no doubt that Nelda was wide awake. The others were shocked by her story.

Rod Havelock was very disturbed and said, "It's a fact now that you have one or more enemies aboard, Nelda. So don't ever go anywhere alone, or stay in the cabin by yourself. You might be in grave danger!"

The girl promised to do what he said, and Nancy assured her that she and her friends would certainly protect her. Then she told how she and Rod had brought her trunk from the hold and would put the mystery trunk into the wardrobe of cabin one thirty.

This was accomplished with the help of the two girls, then Rod locked the connecting door from one twenty-eight to one thirty and handed the girls the keys.

"Good night," he said, "although it's really morning." He looked at his wrist watch. "Only three hours sleep for me. I'd better go."

When he had left, the girls restored the keys to their hiding place in the wardrobe. Nancy's trunk was shoved under the bed, where the other one had been, then Nelda heaved a sigh of relief. "I feel so much better now!"

Nancy smiled. "I'm glad. Let's get some sleep. I'll unpack in the morning, because I'm much too weary now."

As Bess and Nelda settled under the covers, Nancy began to undress. Suddenly Bess said, "I just had a horrible thought. That man who telephoned might have broken in here and thought I was Nelda! He would have thrown me overboard by mistake!"

Nancy tried to make light of the matter, but the words seemed to stick in her throat. She realized it could have happened!

CHAPTER VIII

Sign Language

AFTER breakfast Nancy, Bess, and Nelda hurried back to their cabin. It had just been tidied by Heinrich. He was about to leave, but stood staring at Nancy's brass-bound trunk. Upon seeing the girls, he said, "Good morning, ladies," and quickly left the cabin.

"Snooping again," Bess remarked.

Nancy wondered if the steward realized it was a different trunk from the one that had been under her bed before. She mentioned this to the others.

"Oh, I'm sure he noticed," Nelda said. "I just wonder if he'll tell others."

George said, "I have never trusted that man. I predict that one of these days we're going to find out he has something to do with the mystery."

"He.could be an informer and nothing more," Nancy said.

Within minutes there was a knock on the door. Nancy opened it. Lou, the locksmith, stood there. He smiled, said good morning, and added, "I brought something unique to show you."

He stepped into the room and took a compli-cated-looking lock with no lid from his pocket. Then he produced a key with many notches in it. "I thought you young ladies might be interested in seeing this master key and lock. It's something new. I picked it up in Rotterdam just before we left."

To Nancy, the mechanism of the lock looked like the intricate workings of a very fine watch. She mentioned this to Lou.

"You're right," he said. "And they're just about as hard to devise, maybe harder."

Nelda said, "Please show us how the key works."

Lou inserted it into the keyhole, then said, "Now watch carefully."

The girls' eyebrows raised in admiration as he turned the key and the various parts began to move—the pins, tumbler, springs, the driver spool, bolt spring, cam, and finally the roller bolt. He explained each part, opening and closing the lock several times.

"Fabulous!" Bess remarked. "It would take a great brain to figure this out." She giggled. "Not one like mine."

"This key is a master key," the locksmith went

on, "but not a simple one like some." He said that probably only six locks were made like this one, but each slightly different. "This particular key, though, could open all of them," he added.

Nelda asked, "Could anyone order this lock and key?"

"Oh yes," Lou replied.

All the time he had been demonstrating the unusual lock in his hands, he was stealing glances at Nancy's trunk under her bed. Nancy assumed he suspected it was different from the one for which he had made the key. She was afraid he might question her about it.

"If he does, how should I answer him?" she thought. Luckily, Lou said nothing.

Nancy wondered whether or not he had come to the girls' cabin of his own volition. Or had Heinrich reported his suspicions to the locksmith and requested that he look for himself? Showing off a lock and key would be a perfect cover-up.

A few minutes later Lou left. At once the three girls began to discuss his visit. All wondered if he had brought the unique lock because he thought they would be interested. Or was this just an excuse to look at the brass-bound trunk in cabin one twenty-eight?

Bess checked her watch. "Visiting hours at the infirmary are beginning," she said. "Let's go down to see George. She'll want to know what's been happening while she's been gone."

"Good idea," Nancy agreed.

The three girls stepped into the corridor, locked their cabin door, and hurried away. They found George looking healthy and feeling much better. She was eager to leave the hospital.

"Tell me everything you've been doing," she begged. "Knowing Nancy Drew, I'm sure I've missed a lot of excitement."

In whispers, the other three girls took turns bringing George up-to-date on all that had taken place during the past twenty-four hours. Several times the patient's eyes opened wide and once her lower jaw dropped when she heard about the dire threat to Nelda.

"To think I missed all this!" George groaned, as Nancy finished the story. "But I won't be out of things much longer. The doctor says I may leave here just before dinner tonight!"

"Wonderful!" said Bess.

"I have a request," George added.

"What's that?" Nancy asked.

George replied, "Would you mind waiting until I can be with you before you open the mystery trunk and make a closer examination of the contents?"

The three girls agreed and then said good-by. They noticed an open magazine lying upside down on her bed and assumed that she had been reading it. They were sure the hours would pass quickly until dinnertime.

On the way to the upper deck Nelda asked, "What do you suggest we do in the meantime? Some more sleuthing?"

"How about having some fun?" Bess answered promptly. "I'm tired of being so serious. We can swim and play shuffleboard and do lots of other things outdoors. Besides, I want to get some more sun tan before we get back home."

The girls decided to play shuffleboard first and went to the top deck. They found a court that was not being used and began to play.

Presently Bess said, "Oh, Nelda, you're just too good!"

The girl from Johannesburg laughed and admitted that she often played this game at home.

"My father is a real challenger, and I learned many points from him," Nelda explained.

Nancy had been glancing around at other players and passengers stretched out in deck chairs, enjoying the sun. Her eyes lighted on one man seated by himself in a corner. To her amazement he was using the sign language of deaf people.

"He must be practicing," the girl thought to herself.

Interested at once, Nancy excused herself from the shuffleboard game and moved a little closer to the man. Could he be the same person who had been "talking" to the man on the dock at Rotterdam—the one who had been given the warning message: –EWARE NANCY DREW AND NE?

The girl detective was able to figure out parts of the words the man was practicing. The first one was CREW, the second CAN. The third word had four letters in it, the second one being E. The fourth word had two letters she did not know, but the last two were ND.

As Nancy watched the last word, she smiled with excitement. She had detected NEC—ACE. "It must mean necklace!" she thought. "And that could mean stolen jewelry!"

More eager than ever to find out something about this passenger, she moved a little closer. He had stopped practicing and now lay back in his deck chair, staring out over the ocean. It was calm and almost waveless.

Nancy walked up to the man. "Pardon me," she said. "I saw you practicing the finger language. Are you deaf?" If he was, she knew he could probably read her lips and understand the question.

To her surprise, the man shook his head. "No, I'm not deaf. I can hear very well. I'm on my way to New York to meet my father, who is deaf. I thought I'd surprise him by learning the finger alphabet he has to use now."

"That's very nice," Nancy said. She felt, however, that the man was not speaking the truth. Why was he lying?

He looked at her sharply. "Do you understand the finger language?" he asked.

"Oh, no," Nancy replied. "I once learned to spell my own name, that's all."

The stranger rose suddenly, as if he did not want to converse any longer with Nancy. Excusing himself, he walked off quickly.

Nancy decided to follow him and see if she could find out who he was. She came back to the shuffleboard court and paused a second to speak to the girls.

"I'm on that man's trail. I'm going to follow him and see if I can learn anything about him."

She went on and had no trouble keeping the stranger in sight. He seemed to be in a hurry and did not look back.

The man headed straight toward cabin one twenty-eight! As he paused there, Heinrich came up to him. Nancy moved as close as she dared but turned into an adjoining corridor, hoping she could see and hear what went on between the two men.

To her disappointment, they spoke in very low voices. Nancy could not make out their conversation. She saw the stranger hand Heinrich a bill, and after a few more words he walked off in the opposite direction.

Nancy hurried forward and caught up with the steward, wondering why the stranger had handed him the money. Was he bribing Heinrich for some reason? If so, what? Did it have anything to do with cabin one twenty-eight?

CHAPTER IX

The Sealed Tray

WHEN Nancy reached Heinrich, she asked him who the man was. The steward looked a little frightened, but said his name was Mr. August.

"He was on the last trip of this ship. I was his steward."

Nancy smiled. "How nice of him to come and talk to you!" As she said this, she watched Heinrich's face closely.

The steward showed no sign of guilt. He merely replied, "I bought some special candy for Mr. August in Holland and he just came to pay me for it."

Nancy wondered if Heinrich was telling the truth. Was the man really Mr. August, and what cabin was he occupying? She decided to look at the passenger list, which had been delivered to each room.

Glancing at the A's in the folder, she spotted a Mr. Otto August.

"He must be the one!" she thought.

No cabin number was given, but the young detective decided to try to find it out anyway. She hurried to the purser's office and asked Rod Havelock for August's room number.

The assistant purser gave her a long look, then smiled. "I'm sorry, but it's against the rules of the *Winschoten* to give out the cabin number of anyone aboard."

Nancy looked crestfallen. "Oh, dear! It's really important that I find out." Now she would have to try some other way to glean the information.

Havelock glanced at her, then said, "I suggest that you follow me."

Speaking to another man at the desk, he left his post, came out through a side door, and walked up one of the corridors. Nancy followed, but instinct told her not to catch up to him. She was sure he had something in mind that would help her learn more about the mysterious Mr. Otto August.

In a few moments the assistant purser turned into another corridor, then went up a stairway. She followed a few yards behind. Rod did not slow his pace until they had gone two decks above. Then, once more, he entered a corridor and proceeded toward the middle of the ship. Suddenly he began to walk more slowly, and finally paused for a few seconds in front of cabin four twenty-five. Then he went on without turning to speak to her.

Nancy smiled. "This must be Otto August's cabin! I wonder if he has a roommate. I'll have to figure this out."

For a moment she was tempted to try to locate the steward who serviced this cabin. Then she decided it would be best not to reveal that she had been there. "But I'll work on this some more."

She turned back, retraced her steps, and proceeded directly to where she had left her friends on the sports deck.

"What's up?" Bess asked her.

"I'll tell you all about it later," Nancy promised.

Nelda said she was tired of the deck sports. "Let's go swimming," she suggested.

The other girls agreed and went at once to their cabin. While they were changing into bathing suits, Nancy told them how she had found out about Otto August.

"He sat by himself and was practicing the sign language. I spoke to him. He's not deaf. He said he was practicing the finger language in order to 'talk' to his father in New York. I also found out he's staying in cabin four twenty-five."

Nelda expressed her admiration for the girl detective's astute sleuthing. "You amaze me, Nancy," she said.

The young detective smiled and said, "Don't give me too much praise until I solve your mystery and the mystery of the brass-bound trunk."

The girls went to the pool. A group of teen-age

girls had gathered around four college boys. They waved to Nancy and her friends as they approached them.

A red-haired boy said to Nancy, "You certainly have been avoiding us lately!"

Nancy laughed. "We don't even know you!"

"That's no reason to avoid us," the boy went on. "My name is Al, and my friends here are Bruce, Chipper, and Tubby over there." He pointed to a chubby boy with blond, curly hair.

The girls laughed and introduced themselves.

"We're glad we finally met you," Al said with a grin. "And now that you know us, how about a race in the pool?"

"You fellows against us?" Bess asked. "That wouldn't be fair."

"Never accuse Al of being unfair," the cheerful redhead said. "We'll make girl-boy teams, of course. I'll take Nancy Drew as a partner. Okay with you, Nancy?"

"Why not?" Nancy could not help but like the friendly boy.

Dark-haired Bruce chose Bess, while Chipper teamed up with Nelda.

Tubby made a face. "As always, poor Tubby winds up without a girl," he said good-naturedly. "But I don't mind. I'll time you people. Al, give me your stop watch, will you please?"

"Over there in my jacket pocket. Tub, you're a good sport!"

"Since the pool is small, how about four laps apiece?" Chipper suggested.

"Okay," Al said. "Swim any style you want. Girls, you start. Ladies first, of course!"

The three girls lined up and when Tubby gave the signal, they dived in. Nancy was off to a good start and led in the first two laps. Then Nelda put on an extra burst of speed and almost caught up to her by the time they finished their stretch. Bess lagged behind slightly. Now the boys dived in. All the girls at the pool cheered them on with excited screams.

"Come on, Al! Hurry up!" Nancy called out.

Chipper went into a turn, which he executed beautifully, gaining some time. "Great, Chipper!" Nelda cried. "We'll make it yet!"

"Better hurry, Chipper," a teen-age boy teased. "A kiss for the winner!"

Chipper was swimming through the water so fast that he looked like a dark streak in the waves. Other people gathered and watched the meet.

One woman called out, "This is the most fun I've seen since I climbed aboard!"

Chipper came in first, half a length before Al, and the rest gathered around him to congratulate him and Nelda for winning the competition. The swimmers were breathing heavily and sat down to rest.

Sara Jane Ramsey came over and joined Nancy. "You're a marvelous swimmer," she said.

"Oh, thank you," Nancy replied.

Sara stared at Nancy's swimsuit. "It's a Lochinvar Special, isn't it?" she asked.

Before Nancy had a chance to answer Bess put in, "Yes, Nancy bought it in Switzerland."

"Oh," said Sara Jane, "then you found your trunk? Lucky you!"

"Yes," Nancy said. "It had been delivered to the hold instead of my cabin, but it was finally found."

As she spoke, she happened to glance at a man standing nearby. *Otto August!*

She was sure he had overheard the conversation. "Well," Nancy thought, "that's all right. Now he'll think his trunk is in the hold instead of mine, so he won't come into our cabin looking for it. At least I hope that's what he'll think!"

She told her friends she was going to get out of her wet swimsuit. Bess and Nelda went with her. While changing, they discussed Sara Jane Ramsey and her inadvertent remark. She had advertised to those standing around that Nancy's trunk was now in one twenty-eight.

Nancy said to the other girls, "Did you notice that older man standing nearby? Medium height, with a receding blond hairline? He's Otto August!"

Nelda looked frightened. "Do you think he's connected with the jewel robbery in Johannesburg?" she asked Nancy.

The girl detective admitted that she suspected him strongly.

The telephone rang, and Nancy picked it up. George was calling from the infirmary.

"How do you feel?" Nancy asked her. "Will you be out by tonight?"

"Sure. I feel fine. But I need my mice."

"What?"

George laughed. "The mice I want to sew on my costume, Nancy. Will one of you please bring me the nightie and the mice? They're already cut out. They're in a plastic bag in my suitcase, together with thread and needle."

"Sure, George, we'll get them to you," Nancy said. She hung up.

The errand was completed and the afternoon seemed to pass quickly. At about five o'clock there was a tap on their door. George had arrived! She looked rested and healthy and declared she felt great. She showed them her nightie.

"Cute," said Bess. "But those mice look too real to suit me!"

"Did anything exciting happen this afternoon?" George asked.

Nancy related the events and George remarked in praise, "You don't waste a minute, do you, Nancy? So you think Otto August is a suspect."

The young sleuth nodded. Then she told George that after the evening festivities were over, they would open the mystery trunk.

"I hope we find a treasure inside," George said.

After dinner the four girls returned to one twenty-eight and put on their masquerade costumes. They entered the parade. George received the first prize in the women's section. Her long, old-fashioned nightie with the mice on it brought laughter and applause.

The candle she was carrying flickered jauntily as she went up to receive her trophy. It was a tiny replica of the *Winschoten,* and contained some delightful perfume.

As soon as all the prizes had been given out, the band began to play a lively dance number. Rod Havelock, who had been watching closely, came up to claim Nancy and was only a second ahead of Al.

"I guess I'd better get my dances in early," the assistant purser teased. "I see I have a handsome rival."

Nancy laughed as they glided off. "I'm glad you did, because I must ask you a question. We are planning to open the mystery trunk tonight after this party is over. Will you come and help us investigate it?"

"You bet I will," Rod replied. "I can tell you now that the dancing will end at eleven o'clock sharp. Shall we say eleven-fifteen in your room?"

"Perfect," Nancy agreed.

At this moment the music ended. Others came

up to talk to the couple, and presently Al made his way toward Nancy. "May I have the next dance?" he asked.

The whole evening was a joyful one for Nancy and her friends. They were claimed for every dance. Al asked the girl detective if she would accompany him to the lavish table of food that had been set up on the deck outside.

She went along and they found Bess, George, and Nelda there with Bruce, Chipper, and Tubby.

"Hey, have some of those delicious meatballs!" Tubby recommended.

"Now, Tub, I thought you were staying away from all this fattening stuff?" Chipper teased.

"Well, I had to try a little of each!" Tubby defended himself.

When the music began to play again, Al asked Nancy to dance.

"Sure, I'd like to," she said.

"I'm glad you would," Al commented. "Next to football, dancing is my favorite pastime."

At eleven o'clock when the band was playing the final number, the boys asked the girls to go to another part of the ship, where there would be dancing till after midnight.

"I'd better not," George said. "Remember, I just came out of the hospital and the doctor told me to take it easy."

"Some other time," Nancy promised Al, who was disappointed. "Tonight we have to take care of George."

The girls went to cabin one twenty-eight. A few minutes later Rod Havelock arrived. They locked the room on the inside, so no one could use a passkey to intrude.

"All set?" Rod asked.

"We certainly are," Nancy replied and led the way to the adjoining room. She switched on the light, then realized that anyone passing by in the corridor could see a crack of light underneath the door.

She went to the bathroom, took a long Turkish towel, unfolded it, then rolled it lengthwise and laid it against the door on the floor.

"Now no one will suspect we're in here," she whispered to the others. "Also, I suggest we speak in very low tones."

"Right," Rod said. He unlocked the wardrobe and hauled out the mystery trunk. He set it in the middle of the floor and Nancy now used the key Lou, the locksmith, had made to open it. She swung back the lid and the girls took out the contents.

"I hope Mr. X doesn't expect us to hang up his suits properly," Bess giggled, and she proceeded to pile the clothes on the bed.

"You know, these look as if they're different sizes," George observed. "Those brown pants seem much shorter than the ones for that gray suit over there."

"Maybe he supplies his whole gang with outfits," Rod suggested.

When the trunk was empty, Nancy tapped all sides of it. Then she tried the bottom, pressing hard on every inch. Suddenly she smiled. "I think this is a false bottom!" she announced.

"Really?" George asked in a hoarse whisper. "Can you tell for sure?"

"It sounds that way," Nancy replied and studied the flowered paper that lined the entire trunk.

"Bess, would you mind bringing me my flashlight?" she requested.

Bess hurried into one twenty-eight to get Nancy's light from a drawer. She handed it to the young sleuth, who immediately beamed the flashlight on the flowered paper.

"There's a well-disguised seam here," Nancy said, pointing. "Maybe I can get the paper off without ruining it."

"How?" George asked.

Nancy said, "Let's try soaking it to see if we can loosen it."

Bess asked, "Why bother?"

Nelda answered, "We don't want to alert the owner that we have tampered with his property, even though we suspect him."

By this time, George had obtained a Turkish

towel from the bathroom, soaked it, and brought it to Nancy. The plan worked and in a few minutes the girl detective was able to peel off the flowered paper from the bottom of the trunk.

The others crowded around to look at what was underneath. They stared in surprise.

"A wooden tray!" Bess exclaimed. "With a lid!"

"Which doesn't open," Nancy said in disappointment, as she and Rod tried it unsuccessfully. Suddenly Nancy held up her hand. "Shh!"

There was complete silence for a few seconds.

"What is it?" George whispered.

"I thought I heard a noise outside. I don't know whether it was here or at the door of cabin one twenty-eight!"

"What shall we do?" Bess asked.

"I think I'd better investigate," Rod decided. "You stay here and be very quiet."

"Wouldn't it be better if I went out to look?" Nancy said. "You could be right behind me and back me up in case of trouble."

"Okay," Rod agreed, and the two tiptoed into cabin one twenty-eight through the connecting doors. Nancy opened the door and looked out into the corridor. There was no one in sight!

"I could have sworn I heard someone out here!" Nancy said. "Whoever it was must have hurried off while we were discussing what to do!"

"Well, let's get back to the trunk," Rod sug-

"This trunk has a false bottom!" Nancy exclaimed.

gested. They locked the door again and joined the others, who had discovered a series of small holes across the top of the tray.

"They must be keyholes," Nancy suggested. "Now what are we going to do?"

Nelda answered, "Why don't we call my uncle? I'm sure he can help us."

The others agreed and urged her to call the captain at once.

He answered immediately, but said he was in bed. His niece told him what Nancy had discovered in the mystery trunk.

"Amazing!" he replied, "This should be investigated further. I'll be right down!"

CHAPTER X

Dutch Dials

CAPTAIN Detweiler arrived in a short time. He gazed for several seconds at the hidden tray Nancy had discovered. He was as eager as the others to open it and learn what it contained.

Nancy asked him about Lou, the locksmith. "We've had no luck trying to open it. Do you trust him fully?"

The captain smiled. "I've known Lou for many, many years. He's as honest and faithful as a good Dutch windmill."

He turned to Rod Havelock. "Please go down and get Lou. Tell him I want him up here right away with a bag of tools and devices to open locks, unusual locks, that is."

"Shall I wake him if he's asleep?" the assistant purser asked.

"Yes. It's very important, but he's not to mention it to anyone."

Havelock left at once. He did, indeed, find the locksmith sound asleep. After hearing the urgent message, Lou dressed quickly and the two men returned to the girls' cabin, where the captain explained the problem.

"I thought all along there was something funny about that trunk," Lou said.

"There is," Captain Detweiler admitted and swore the man to secrecy. Then the girls showed Lou the tray they had found in the mystery trunk.

The locksmith was amazed. Before he began working on it, he studied the tray with the four small holes across the top of the lid for a couple of minutes. Then he opened his bag of tools. The others watched eagerly as he tried round keys, thin flat ones, and strange-looking corrugated keys. Nothing would open the lid of the tray.

Lou now tried thin rods. When these failed in all four of the tiny openings, he inserted slender wires. He wiggled them, frowning more deeply with each attempt.

Finally the frustrated locksmith began to mutter to himself in Dutch. Nancy could not understand any of it, so Nelda translated and whispered in her ear.

"He is saying, 'Very clever, very clever. But I will conquer this thing yet!'"

Nancy smiled and rooted even harder for Lou. He kept shaking his head so much that Bess whispered to Nelda, "If he keeps this up, his head will fall off!"

At this point Nancy decided to get her magnifying glass and examine the top of the tray thoroughly. She brought it from her own trunk and scrutinized each inch of the tray. Along the bottom of the lid she could see letters and figures indistinctly.

"They might be a clue on how to open this!" she said. "Lou, please take this glass and look at the writing. Perhaps it gives instructions on how to proceed."

Lou took the glass and studied the marks intently for several seconds. Suddenly he smiled. "You're right!" he said. "This is in Dutch and says *'Een rechts, twee links, een naar boven, drie naar beneden.'* "

"How exciting!" Nelda exclaimed. "That means one right, two left, one up, and three down."

Lou was still studying the directions. Finally he said, "This tray may have a dial inside the lid like those used on safes in banks. Yes, it must be like that."

He took one of the wires, bent it at one end into a loop, and inserted it into the first hole. Then he put his ear down to listen for any response from the lock. When there was none, he pushed the wire to the right. Apparently he heard some kind of sound. He withdrew the wire and pushed it to the left, then back and to the left again. He now pulled the wire almost to the top, then lowered it three times. There was an audible *click!*

As everyone waited breathlessly, Lou lifted the lid off the tray. The girls tried hard not to shout, expressing their delight in hushed voices. Captain Detweiler patted the locksmith on the shoulder. "Great work, Lou," he said.

The contents of the tray were covered with a cloth, which Nancy was urged to take off. As she did, a series of small suede pouches became visible.

"What do you think is in them?" Bess whispered.

Nancy turned to the captain. "I feel you should have the honor of opening the first pouch," she said.

The officer smiled. "No. You're the one who is solving this mystery. You open it!"

Nancy did, and out rolled a fair-sized sapphire. It glinted in the light.

"I don't believe it!" George whispered. "Hurry up and open the rest!"

Nancy insisted that there were plenty of pouches and each person in the cabin should open one of them. As they did, diamonds, rubies, topazes, and garnets were revealed.

The group were speechless. Finally Captain Detweiler said, "There's no question but that whoever hid these in the trunk expected to smuggle them into the United States!"

Bess asked, "What are you going to do with them?"

Rod Havelock suggested that they be taken to the ship's safe in the purser's office.

But the captain had another idea. "I have a very fine secret safe in my quarters. I think the jewels should be put in there. No one but the people in this room will know about them."

Nancy asked, "Can you put all of them away at once without anyone seeing you?"

The officer smiled. "Indeed, I can. Rod will stuff his pockets with pouches, and I'll stuff mine. Then we'll go up to my quarters immediately."

He turned to the locksmith. "Lou, you have been a wonderful help, and I know you're happy to think that you've been able to uncover apparently smuggled gems."

The locksmith smiled. "You know you can rely on me, sir." He packed his tools, said good night, and left the cabin.

"What a nice man he is," Nancy said. "And to think I was once suspicious of him."

In a few minutes Captain Detweiler and the assistant purser also went off, their pockets bulging.

The girls put back the tray, piled the suits and work clothes into the mystery trunk, and locked it.

"Come on, Nelda, help me lift this into the wardrobe again," Nancy said.

"Certainly."

When the trunk was safely hidden, Nelda asked, "What are we going to do with this soaking wet flowered paper?"

In her haste to uncover the tray, Nancy had laid the sheets near the porthole window.

"They'll have to dry before we can paste them back," Nancy responded.

She looked around for a place to hide the paper and concluded that underneath the bed was the best spot. "I'll replace them when they're dried," she said. The girl detective added that she hoped the paper would not wrinkle or shrink. If so, it would be a dead giveaway should the suspect locate the trunk and examine it.

"Then we'd really be in trouble," Bess remarked.

"But nothing compared to the trouble the jewel thief will be in," George predicted.

Nelda had a faraway look in her eyes. Nancy guessed that the words "jewel thieves" had brought painful memories to her. The accusation against her had never been cleared up.

"Oh, if only we could find that diamond bracelet," Nancy thought.

The girls carefully slipped the paper under the bed to dry; then they put out the lights and went next door into their own cabin. Bess made sure all the doors were locked.

"I wonder what those gems are worth," George said. "There were so many I didn't even count them."

"A fortune, no doubt," Bess added. "I'd love to own just one or two of them!"

"It's dreadfully late," Nancy said with a yawn.

George nodded. "What an evening we've had," she said.

"Yes, and you're right out of the infirmary," Bess remarked. "You were supposed to take it easy!"

George giggled. "We'd better get out of these costumes and get to bed."

In the excitement all of them had forgotten that they were still in their strange-looking clothes.

"Wait!" Bess said. "I want to take a picture of each of you!" She dashed for her camera and inserted flash cubes.

"You can take one of me with my candle right in front of the bed," George said. "It's the perfect background!"

Bess did, then had the others pose for a photograph. When she was finished, Nancy took one of Bess.

"George, I dare you to send one of these mouse pictures to your friend Burt!" Bess teased her cousin.

George made a face. "I never want him to see me like that!"

"Why not? You won first prize!"

"Sure. For the funniest-looking creature on board. Hardly something you would want to advertise to your boyfriend."

Finally the four girls climbed into bed. They had hardly closed their eyes, when the phone rang. Sleepily Nancy picked it up. "Hello?"

"Nancy?" a man's voice answered. "This is Rod Havelock. Is your door locked safely from the inside?"

"Yes."

"Good," the assistant purser said. "On the way upstairs the captain and I were attacked by two masked men. One of them said, "We know Nancy Drew has put you up to something. What's in your pockets?""

By this time Nancy was wide awake, and frightened. "Oh, Rod!" she exclaimed, "are you and the captain all right? And did the men get the pouches?"

CHAPTER XI

Bits of Evidence

In reply to Nancy's excited question, Rod Havelock chuckled. "Yes, we're okay. We weren't seriously hurt except for a few black-and-blue marks."

"Who attacked you?"

"Two men. Actually we got the better of them," Rod said, "because both of them lost their balance and fell down the flight of stairs. You see, they were waiting at the top in one of the cross corridors and jumped us just as we came up."

"What about the pouches?" Nancy asked.

"They're safe and intact. We didn't lose any time getting to the captain's cabin with them," Rod replied.

Nancy heaved a sigh of relief. "I'm glad that you're all right and that you saved the pouches."

"Thank you," Havelock said. He laughed softly. "You'll probably be relieved to know that

I'm spending the rest of the night with the captain."

"I'm glad," Nancy said.

Havelock told her that the ship's watchmen had been alerted, but so far they had reported seeing no one.

"Those attackers," Nancy said, "must have watched you and the captain come into our cabin and then waited until just before you left. I'll bet they're the same two who came into our room to claim the mystery trunk!"

"Probably," Rod agreed.

"I'll go right out and see if they left any clues," Nancy offered.

"Oh, no!" Havelock insisted. "Don't leave your cabin now! Those people know you're involved in this mystery, and you mustn't take any chances. At this hour, nearly everyone is asleep, and if something were to happen to you, you might not get help in time."

"I suppose you're right," Nancy admitted. She promised to go to bed and wait until morning before doing any sleuthing. She asked, "What were your attackers wearing?"

"Bathrobes and black hoods that came down over their entire faces."

"Did they wear gloves?" the girl detective inquired.

"No, they didn't."

"How about shoes?"

Rod said that both men wore dark-colored slippers. "One masked man had on a garnet-colored robe, the other a navy-blue one with pale-blue piping."

"On which stairway were you attacked?" Nancy asked.

Rod said, "On the most forward one, leading from your deck up to the top, where the captain's quarters are."

Nancy thought about this a moment, then suddenly was conscience-stricken because she was keeping Havelock from going to bed. "He must be weary after his encounter with the attackers!" she chided herself. She apologized for keeping him on the phone so long and said, "Thanks for calling me. I'll be in touch. Have a good rest."

Nancy herself fell into a fitful sleep. She dreamed that while she was looking for clues on the deck she found a tiny diamond glittering in one of the lounge chairs. As she approached it, the diamond became larger and brighter until it filled the whole chair.

Nancy wanted to call out to her friends, but her voice was gone! The brightness of the stone became so intense that it hurt her eyes and she woke up. She sat upright in her bed and checked her watch. It was just six o'clock. "No use in going back to sleep," Nancy thought. "Next time I'll probably dream about a killer ruby!"

She dressed quickly without disturbing the

others, took her flashlight, and left the cabin. She
locked the door from the outside, then, without
any trouble, found the stairway where the attackers had been.

The steps were carpeted. She played her flashlight thoroughly on each one as she ascended.
About halfway up, the girl detective saw a tiny
piece of black cloth lying on the carpet. She
picked it up and examined the fragment thoroughly under her flashlight. "I wonder if this
could possibly have been torn from one of the
men's masks," she speculated.

Nancy kept examining the stairway until she
was only three steps from the top. Suddenly her
eyes lighted on a piece of paper. It was rolled into
a tiny ball. The girl picked it up and straightened
it out. Then she looked at it in amazement. It was
part of a drawing of a diamond bracelet! "Wow!"
she said to herself. "What a find!"

The diamonds were a silver color against a
black background, and the design was beautiful
in its striking simplicity. In one corner of the paper was a very faint line.

As the young sleuth stared at it, she wondered
whether the line would give some real information if she looked at it under a magnifying glass.
She put both the paper and the cloth into a
pocket and ascended the stairs, going all the way
to the top deck. She came across nothing else of
importance.

"I'd better get back to my cabin," Nancy decided, "and look at this paper under my magnifying glass."

On the way she almost bumped into a cleaning man as she turned a corner. He said to her, "It is too early for you to be up."

"Oh, I like to get up early," Nancy replied and hurried off.

By the time she let herself into cabin one twenty-eight, the other girls were awake. They demanded to know where she had been and why. When she told them, and pulled the evidence from her pocket, they were amazed.

Nancy went to get her magnifying glass and studied both the cloth and the piece of black paper. The cloth revealed no clues, but the line on the paper turned into letters. She could just read the indistinct letters of the word *Longstreet*.

"Do you think that's an address?" Bess suggested.

"Could be the name of the manufacturer who makes this odd black paper," Nelda put in.

"Or the name of the person for whom the bracelet was created," Nancy said.

"Or for that matter, it could be the name of the designer," Bess went on.

Nancy started to laugh. "Hold it! As detectives, we must not get carried away with guesses. Let's try to find out the facts!"

There was silence. Nancy sighed. "Perhaps the

captain could give us an idea. Let's go to see him after breakfast."

When the girls arrived at his quarters, they were told by a junior officer that Captain Detweiler would be busy until eleven-thirty.

Nancy decided to call at the purser's counter and show Rod her discoveries.

Rod Havelock was astounded at the bits of evidence the young sleuth had found. He examined them carefully. Finally he said, "This piece of black material could have been torn from one of the masks. When the captain and I were fighting off those two men, I yanked one fellow's mask down so far that I was sure he couldn't see through the eyeholes. Probably that's why he lost his balance and fell down the stairs."

Nancy asked him if he had any suggestions about the black paper with part of a sketch of a diamond bracelet and the word *Longstreet* on it.

"Sorry, but on that I can't help you," Rod replied.

Nancy noticed that several people were waiting to ask the assistant purser questions, so she decided to leave. When she returned to cabin one twenty-eight, she found her companions looking in their suitcases for Ping-Pong balls.

George said, "We hoped you'd return in time to play doubles with us."

Nancy agreed and the four girls hurried to the sports deck. They twirled their paddles for a choice of partners. Bess and Nancy would play against George and Nelda.

Nelda giggled. "I hope I'll do all right," she said. "I haven't played in a couple of years and I'm rather out of practice."

"Don't worry," George said. "Come on, you start."

Nelda hit a low serve that caught Nancy by surprise. She missed it. Nancy laughed. "Nelda, I'd hate to play against you when you're *not* out of practice!"

George and Nelda won the first game, but Nancy and Bess made up for it in the next one. A crowd gathered to watch the match, and soon each team had its own cheering section.

"Come on, Nancy, let's have a good—oh, oh, it just skimmed the net!"

"No way George could get that!" a sympathetic boy called, while someone else complimented the girl on her tricky shot.

Nancy and Bess won again, and George and Nelda held a short war council. "Bess is a little weak on her backhand," George whispered. "Take advantage of it!"

Nelda did and the game went to her and George. Nancy glanced at her watch. They would just have enough time for one more before she would go to the captain's quarters. The score was very close but finally George and Nelda won.

"Congratulations!" Nancy called out, and the

onlookers clapped. "Now I must leave you and keep my date. Nelda, would you like to come along?"

"Indeed I would," the girl from Johannesburg replied.

The captain opened the door. "Good morning, girls," he said. "Please sit down and tell me your latest news. I know you must have some or you wouldn't have come to see me, right?"

"Well, I did examine the area where you and Mr. Havelock had trouble last night," Nancy said. "I found these clues." She handed the evidence to the captain.

"What is—well, this is amazing!" the man exclaimed. "Do you believe this piece of cloth is from one of the men's masks?"

"It might be," Nancy said. "What do you think of the drawing? That line at the bottom spells *Longstreet* under a microscope."

Captain Detweiler whistled. "Longstreet is the name of a famous jewelry firm in England. I understand they have branches in many cities all over the world." Both girls were astounded by this revelation. But even more so when the captain continued, "A few weeks ago there was a robbery at the English branch of Longstreet's in London."

At once the young detective asked, "Captain Detweiler, do you think our mystery brass-bound trunk could be carrying some of those jewels?"

"That's entirely possible," the captain replied. "It might be very hard to prove, however. All the stones in the pouches have been taken out of their settings."

"Isn't that often done by thieves?" Nancy asked.

The captain nodded. "Yes, and for precisely that reason. It makes the loot hard to identify."

"If only he had left some pieces intact!" Nelda said with a sigh.

Nancy was silent for a few seconds. Suddenly she said, "Maybe we should check out that trunk again. Perhaps it holds some more secrets!"

CHAPTER XII

Little Bobby's Clue

"YES, by all means, search further in the mystery trunk," Captain Detweiler told Nancy and Nelda. "Let me give you something that may help." He went to a locker and took out a small tool kit. "Take this with you. It may come in handy," he said.

"Oh, thank you," Nancy said.

The two girls hurried off. On their way back to their cabin, they searched for Bess and George. The cousins were still playing Ping Pong, but were just about to finish.

Nancy told them about Longstreet's. "I think we should search the mysterious trunk further, and the captain agrees with me," she said.

"But Nancy, you had it all emptied out," George said.

"I know, but we never examined the sides,"

Nancy reminded her. "However, I think we'd better wait until tonight, so we won't be disturbed."

The girls decided to walk around for a little while before returning to their cabin. They went to one of the lower decks and marched along briskly. As they neared an inset that led to a lounge, a little boy suddenly jumped out at them. He wore a blask mask.

"Boo!" he shouted at the girls.

To play with him, they pretended to be scared. They ran back and forth around the deck, with the little fellow chasing them. He giggled under the mask and tried to keep it adjusted so he could see through the eyeholes. Finally Nancy decided that they had played with him long enough.

As the girls stopped running, he said, "What's the matter? Can't you take it?"

Nancy ignored the question. Instead she said, "Where did you get that mask?"

She had noticed that a small piece of the black cloth had been ripped out and was sure this mask had been worn by one of the men who had attacked Captain Detweiler and Rod Havelock.

"Oh, I found it," the little boy replied.

George walked up to him and looked stern. "Take off that mask!"

"Why should I?" the little boy retorted. "I found it. It's mine!"

"I'll tell you why," George said firmly. "That mask belongs to a bad man. If he finds you with it, no telling what he may do to you."

The next second the little fellow pulled off the mask. He was cute-looking, and had red hair and freckles. His eyes sparkled mischievously.

"What's your name?" Bess asked him.

"Bobby."

Nancy spoke. "Bobby, where did you find this?"

"Over there on the deck," he replied. "I guess the wind blew it in!"

"I think you should give it to me," Nancy said.

"I—I don't want to. I like it."

"Why don't you let us take it to the captain?" Nancy urged. "You'd be a lot safer without it, Bobby!"

The boy held the mask firmly in one fist, but George's statement about the bad man had scared him a little. Should he give up his prize possession or not?

Suddenly he had an idea. A big grin spread across his face and his eyes twinkled. "Will you give me a quarter for it?" he asked.

Nancy tried hard to suppress a laugh. This little fellow was smart, all right! "That's a lot of money for something the wind blew right into your hands, isn't it?" she asked.

Bobby stood his ground, however. "Take it or leave it!" he announced firmly.

George was getting impatient. "All right," she said and reached into her purse. "Here's your quarter. Now give me that mask and scoot, Bobby!"

The little boy handed her his find, took the money, and laughed. "Ha ha, I made you pay for it!" he called out as he ran off with a big grin.

"Little brat," George scolded. Then she turned to Nancy. "What shall we do after lunch?"

Nelda and Bess suggested sports, including swimming.

"I'd like to play a little game," Nancy said. "It's called FIND OUT HOW THIS MASK GOT HERE."

"How are you going to do that?" Bess inquired.

"I'll try to get some napkins, which weigh about the same. Then we can throw them toward the sea from different points on the ship."

George raised her eyebrows. "And perhaps one will blow right to this spot?"

"That's the idea," Nancy agreed.

First the four girls went to their cabin to see if the torn piece of black cloth fitted the hole in the mask. When Nancy tried it, they all exclaimed in glee! It was a clean tear and matched the empty space exactly.

Nelda sat down on her bed. "I'd like to review this mystery a bit," she said. "The two men who attacked my uncle and Rod Havelock wore masks. One of them dropped a piece of paper with part of a design for a diamond bracelet. The name Longstreet was on the paper. This connects them with the jewel robbery."

"You're right so far," George agreed.

Nelda went on, "Rod Havelock, in fighting his attacker, tore the mask but didn't see his face. He knows the men were wearing dark bathrobes and slippers. Did anyone ever check on that, by the way?"

"Oh, yes," Nancy replied. "The captain told me he asked every cabin steward about them. None reported seeing any garnet or dark-blue robes in the rooms assigned to them. So that clue ends in a blank."

Nelda said, "So our best hope is the mask."

"Definitely," Nancy replied.

As the girls walked toward the dining room, they stopped at the purser's office. Rod Havelock was there and Nancy whispered her latest findings to him.

He raised his eyebrows in surprise. Then he laughed. "Every time I see you, Nancy, you have a new clue to offer."

She and the other girls agreed, then Rod said, "And now I have a surprise of my own. The two bathrobes and slippers were found in one of the bundles of laundry a little while ago!"

"Great!" Nancy exclaimed. "Where?"

"In the corridor opposite cabin two fifteen."

For a moment Nancy was hoping that he would

say four twenty-five, which was Mr. Otto August's room. Then she told herself that should he be guilty, of course he would not leave the telltale articles where they might be traced to him.

Rod said, "The steward in the corridor where the bathrobes and slippers were found was quizzed about the things. He declared he knew nothing about them. Later, when he was collecting the bundles of linen, he realized that one looked rather fat and that the knot in it was pulled taut. So he checked and discovered the bathrobes and slippers he had been questioned about earlier."

"I'd like to look at them," Nancy said. "Perhaps we'll find a clue in the pockets."

"I did it already," Rod said. "I went over everything with a fine-toothed comb, but turned up absolutely nothing."

"Oh, that's too bad," Nancy said, disappointed. "Another clue that ended in a blank."

After lunch Bess said, "If we're going to be up late tonight, how about a nice sun-tan snooze? Let's lie in lounge chairs on the top deck!"

"I'm all for it," Nelda said. "I had too much dessert and I'm in no mood to do anything strenuous right now."

George liked the idea. "You know, I feel the same way."

Nancy was a little disappointed. She had intended to go to work immediately. The girl sleuth wanted to find out where the masks might have been discarded and whether the wind had blown one to the spot where Bobby had found it. But she decided to join the others for a while.

They all put on swimsuits, sun-tan oil, and dark glasses. Then they went to the topmost deck, found lounge chairs, and stretched out.

"Ohhh, that feels good," Bess said and fell asleep within minutes.

George and Nelda dozed off, too, but Nancy kept turning the mystery over and over in her mind. While much had been learned, there was still a lot to be done before the case could be solved.

She stood up and began to walk around idly. Suddenly her attention was drawn to two men seated together in a secluded corner. They both had their backs to the girl, but she thought one of them looked like Otto August!

Nancy went closer. Perhaps she could eavesdrop on them! But after a few minutes she realized the men not only were not speaking to each other, they were not moving. Obviously they were asleep.

"No sense in staying here," Nancy thought. "I'll go downstairs and check the direction and velocity of the wind on the weather charts."

She realized that they had to be the same as those of the previous night for her experiment to work. The men must have thrown the masks from an upper deck down into the ocean so they could not be found as evidence, and they had not expected one of them to be caught by the wind and blown on a lower deck!

The girl smiled to herself. "But they were wrong!" she thought. "And they don't even know it."

Nancy compared the present wind conditions on the posted charts with those of the night before and the early morning hours. To her delight they were the same!

"That'll help us a lot in our test," she decided, and went to the purser's office. Rod Havelock was there.

"Hi, Nancy. What's on your mind?" the young man greeted her.

"Do you think the *Winschoten* could donate a few table napkins for an experiment?" Nancy said. "I would like to know which spot that mask was thrown from."

Rod grinned. "As long as it's connected with the mystery, I'm sure we can spare a few. Find Joe in the dining room and tell him I said to give you some."

"Thank you," Nancy said and walked off.

Joe was a short, dark-haired man who gave her a strange look when she made her request. "Do they have to be any particular color?" he asked.

Nancy laughed. "No they don't. And they don't have to be new, either. Give me the oldest ones you have."

Joe grinned. "Good. You'll get the ones with the holes in them."

When Nancy returned to the top deck with the napkins in her bag, she found her friends still asleep. She left the napkins beside George's chair and, not wanting to disturb the girls, walked over to the spot where the two men had been resting in their deck chairs. They were still there, but now they seemed to be awake. Nancy edged closer. To her amazement, she found them speaking to each other in the finger language!

"Otto August is not deaf," she thought. "Perhaps the other man is. But Rod told me there isn't a deaf person on board!"

Nancy watched, fascinated. She wondered if she would be able to decipher any words. A moment later she stiffened. Otto August's companion had just spelled out her name, DREW!

CHAPTER XIII

Shambles!

NANCY was thunderstruck. Why would the two men talk about her in sign language? And what were they saying?

She watched them intently, wishing they would not go so fast. The girl detective tried hard to read what Otto August was communicating to his friend by filling in with blanks the letters she did not recognize.

Again she caught the words NANCY DREW. Carefully she stepped a little closer, making sure she would still be out of the men's sight. They had paused and put their hands down.

"Oh, I hope they'll go on," Nancy thought.

To her delight, they did resume their conversation. By concentrating very hard, Nancy figured out the next sentence, which read: CREW CAN
—E— —-ND NEC—-ACE.

Nancy tried to substitute several letters for the

blank spaces, and finally came up with: CREW CAN HELP FIND NECKLACE.

Nancy caught her breath. Did they mean the crewmen on the *Winschoten* or some other crew? And were they talking about a stolen necklace?

She watched the men continue in sign language, but they were gesturing at such speed that she could not follow. She emitted a frustrated sigh. "I wish I remembered more of those letters!" she thought. Then she recalled the scene at the dock in Rotterdam. "I suppose these people not only use the finger alphabet when they have to, as they did in the ship-to-pier episode, but as a general means of communication," she thought. "It's a clever way to talk to one another and be sure not to be overheard."

She became more suspicious than ever of Otto August. The man evidently was taking no chances of being overheard or having his conversation picked up by a hidden microphone.

Nancy also thought, "These men must automatically switch to finger language when they talk about their criminal activities."

Suddenly her attention was drawn to the suspects again. They had begun to speak aloud to each other. This proved that August's companion was not deaf. "I wonder who he is," Nancy thought, "and if they're sharing a cabin. No doubt he's one of the jewel thieves."

The men were discussing whether they should go to the snack bar for a drink or wait until later in the afternoon. They grinned at each other, and a few seconds afterwards stood up, buttoned their shirts, and left.

Nancy hurried off because she did not want them to notice her. She went back to where her friends had been lounging, but the girls had left the deck.

"Maybe they felt they'd had enough sun and returned to the cabin to change," Nancy reasoned. "I'd better go there myself and tell them what I've just learned."

She walked down to the lower deck and found Bess, George, and Nelda at the foot of the steps, about to ascend.

"Where have you been?" Bess demanded. "We were worried about you!"

"We looked for you in our cabin, but you weren't there," George added.

"Listen," Nancy told them, "I have great news for you. How would you like to go to the coffee shop? I'm terribly thirsty. While we're having something to drink, I'll tell you about it."

"Good idea," George said, and the others agreed, eager to hear Nancy's story.

They went to the coffee shop, ordered sodas, and sat down at a corner table. While they were sipping the refreshing drinks, Nancy told them she had seen Otto August and a friend conversing in the finger language and spelling her name again.

Nelda frowned. "I don't like this. Those are evil men. Nancy, do be careful."

"I will be. But I haven't told you the whole story." She went on with the message she had figured out.

"Hypers!" George exclaimed, when Nancy had finished. "That's a new way to eavesdrop. Only one hitch. A lot of other words could end with *nd* besides *find,* which could change the meaning of the sentence. It could read: 'CREW CAN HELP WIND NECKLACE—OR BIND.' "

"I know," Nancy admitted. "It's a possibility. But in any case, there is no other meaning about my name. That was clear, and it was used twice."

Bess spoke up. "Obviously they know you're an amateur detective and they're worried about what you might do."

"Maybe so," Nancy said. "By the way, what did you do with the napkins I borrowed from the dining-room steward? I had left them by your chair, George."

"I know." George grinned. "We did a little sleuthing on our own with them."

She explained that they had taken the table napkins and experimented to see where they floated to from various points of the ship.

"Did you come up with any conclusions?" Nancy asked eagerly.

"We certainly did," Bess replied. "One of them came down from the promenade deck right to where little Bobby found the mask."

Nancy was pleased. She added, "After the captain and Rod's attackers fell down the stairs, they walked along the promenade deck and threw the masks overboard."

George nodded. "But why didn't they discard their robes the same way?"

Nelda said with a giggle, "Maybe they weren't wearing any clothes underneath!"

When the girls reached their cabin, Nelda found that the door had been left unlocked.

"Heinrich must have been here and forgotten to lock up," she said, opening the door. A moment later she screamed.

The other girls crowded in close behind her and exclaimed in dismay at the sight before them.

The room was a shambles!

Every drawer had been pulled out and ransacked, all the beds were torn apart, and every bit of luggage had been opened, the contents strewn all over the floor.

Nancy's trunk had been yanked out and unpacked. Her clothes were scattered around.

"This is dreadful!" Nelda burst out. "I wonder if anything was taken?"

There was silence for a few minutes, while each girl looked for her own possessions to see if anything of value had been stolen from her luggage.

Finally Bess spoke. "Those intruders were not looking for jewelry," she said, "at least not my kind of costume jewelry."

Nelda added, "And they weren't searching for money, either. Some extra bills I had hidden in another purse are still here."

"Oh, I'm so upset!" Bess wailed. "All this frightens me, but it's even worse for you, Nancy and Nelda."

"Let's call Heinrich and see what his reaction is," Nancy suggested. "Maybe he can tell us if he noticed anyone here." She picked up the telephone. Moments later the steward arrived.

From the expression on his face they were sure that he was not guilty of taking part in the burglary.

"*Ach! Ach!*" he said, slapping a hand to his forehead. He went on speaking Dutch and the American girls could understand nothing he was saying. They stared at him, puzzled.

"Please tell us what you said in English," Nancy begged him.

Heinrich was greatly disturbed. "I locked this door—I know I did—when I finished working in the room. Someone obviously has a passkey and got in here! Oh, what am I going to do? I know

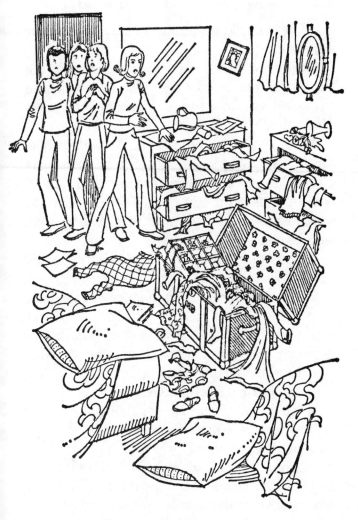

The room was a shambles!

I will be blamed for this. But I really do not know who was here!"

Nancy said she was sorry the steward could not help them, but did not blame him for what had happened. She told him so. "Please don't worry about this."

"Thank you," Heinrich said, and turned around, still shaking his head in disbelief. He closed the door and walked out into the corridor.

George asked the other girls if they felt that the steward was telling the truth. All of them were sure he was.

"In any case," Nancy said, "the intruders did not find what they hoped to."

She stopped speaking and looked out the porthole at the smooth green ocean. For several moments she stood lost in thought. The others glanced at her, sure she would get some idea as to who the would-be thieves were. Certainly they had not been just mischief-makers!

Mischief! At once Nancy thought of little Bobby. This was just the kind of joke he might play on the girls! "But how would he get in here?" she reasoned, and immediately dismissed the thought that Bobby might be the culprit. "This job was more than a prank," she decided.

Suddenly the girl detective turned around. "I just had a horrible idea," she cried out. "If the intruders were the two men who were here before, looking for their trunk, maybe they found it and made a shambles of this room only as a cover-up!"

"Oh, Nancy, you're right!" George said. "Perhaps the other trunk is gone!"

Quickly Nelda got the keys for the adjoining cabin. The girls opened the door leading from one twenty-eight to one thirty and Nancy hurried in, followed by her friends.

The room was undisturbed. Hastily Nancy walked toward the wardrobe. Would the mysterious brass-bound trunk with the initials N.D. on it still be there?

CHAPTER XIV

Stolen Documents

WHEN Nancy peered inside the wardrobe, she exclaimed, "Boy, am I relieved. The mystery trunk is still here!"

"That means," Bess said, "that the intruders have no idea that we have access to this cabin."

Nelda said, "Let's take the trunk out and look for more treasure right now."

"I'd like to," Nancy said, "but first, perhaps we should notify the captain about the break-in."

Nelda nodded. "I'll call my uncle right away," she offered, and went back into their own cabin to use the phone.

The captain was not in his quarters, but a junior officer who was there answered and said he would locate Captain Detweiler so he could take care of the matter at once.

While waiting for him to arrive, the girls carried the mystery trunk from the wardrobe. Nancy unlocked and opened it. Using all her fingers she felt the inside of the lid carefully. Suddenly the young detective paused.

"George, look at this spot," she said, "or rather, feel it. Right over here!"

George knelt on the floor and touched the area Nancy had indicated. "It's a bit lumpy in several places," she announced.

"That's what I thought. I'm inclined to think something is hidden under here!"

Bess and Nelda touched the places and were convinced that Nancy was on the right track.

"Before you take off the paper, though," Bess suggested, "maybe you'd better wait until someone comes about the break-in of our cabin."

"You're right. Let's go back into one twenty-eight and wait for whoever is coming."

The three girls put the trunk back into the wardrobe, then went into their own room. While waiting, they discussed what had happened. George said, "You have two real suspects, Nancy. Otto August and the person he was talking to in the finger language."

Bess agreed with her cousin and said, "I'm sure that they're at least in league with whoever broke in here. In fact, they might have been the ones!"

"That's right," Nancy agreed. "They could have done it after they left the deck and while we were in the coffee shop!"

"But why did they tear up our room?" Nelda

asked. "They could see the trunk wasn't in it."

"Maybe they thought we had found the jewels and hidden them in our cabin," Nancy reasoned.

"And since they didn't find what they came for, they might even try it again," George said with a shudder.

Nancy nodded. "I have a horrible feeling that these people will stop at nothing!" she declared.

Guesses and theories about the subject were propounded by each girl during the next ten minutes. Then a knock sounded on the corridor door. Rod Havelock stood there.

"More trouble down here?" he asked.

"Take a look yourself," Nancy replied.

The assistant purser stepped inside and gasped. "Wow!" he said. "Your intruder did a thorough job of pulling everything apart!"

They closed the door and locked it, then walked forward.

Nancy said, "We haven't found any evidence as to who was here, but we have our suspicions."

"Is anything missing?" Rod asked.

"Not that we know of so far," George replied.

In a low voice Nancy told Rod about their assumption that Otto August and his friend or other gang members who might be on board had been the intruders.

"That would be very hard to prove," the young man said. "You say there is no evidence?"

Nancy now told him what she had figured out from the finger language Otto August and his confederate were using. "But neither man is deaf," she stated. "I think they are part of a ring of jewel thieves who use the finger alphabet as a cover-up to communicate with one another for their operations."

Rod Havelock whistled. "Nancy, you may not have any real evidence, but you're collecting a number of damaging clues."

"I hope they'll lead to something in the end," Nancy said.

"I think we found something concrete in the trunk," George said, and revealed that Nancy and her friends had already started to examine the mysterious piece of luggage again.

"The inside of the lid has a number of lumps in it," Nancy added. "Would you like to help us uncover whatever is there?"

The assistant purser smiled. "I'd like nothing better. Let's go to work!"

Bess spoke up and said she could not live in their room the way it looked. "Suppose George, Nelda, and I clean it up while you two go into cabin one thirty and see what you can find?"

Before entering the adjoining room, Rod suggested that the whole matter be kept secret. Bess revealed that Heinrich already knew about the break-in, but had denied knowing about any intruders and what they were doing. He declared he had not seen anyone come in or leave one twenty-eight after he had tidied the cabin.

Rod said, "He probably has a bit of a guilty feeling, so I doubt that he'd talk. As for the rest of us, shall we say nothing about it to anyone else?"

The others agreed, thinking it a wise idea. Bess grinned, "Mum's the word."

Nancy and Havelock entered the adjoining cabin, took out the brass-bound trunk, and once more Nancy opened it. She showed her companion the uneven places she had discovered on the inside of the lid.

"It seems suspicious," the assistant purser remarked. "I wonder if there are more jewels under this flowered paper."

Nancy said, "I'll get a steaming towel and a little chisel from the tool kit the captain lent me. The towel worked before, so I hope it will this time, too."

"Let's try it," Rod said, and Nancy went to get her equipment.

Very carefully the girl detective began to peel off the paper at one end. The work was slow, so Rod got another towel. Using this and a penknife, he began to loosen the paper on the other end of the lid. Between the two of them, they made quick headway.

Long before they finished, however, Bess, George, and Nelda had straightened out cabin one twenty-eight. They came in to watch.

"You're making progress," Nelda remarked.

Finally the paper was removed in sections. Underneath lay a thin sheet of plywood.

Nancy now chose an awl from the captain's kit and was able to pull up the plywood. Papers and documents tumbled from the lid into the trunk!

"What do you suppose these are?" Bess asked. "Something important?"

Rod picked up one of the papers, spread it out, and looked at the words intently.

"It's in Dutch," he said. "I can read only a little of that language. Part of it is handwritten and I can't figure it out. Nelda, how about your trying to translate it?"

The girl from Johannesburg picked up paper after paper and read the contents. Several times she frowned as she finished one and put it down.

"What do they say?" Bess asked impatiently.

Nelda did not reply at once. She kept going from one document to another. Some seemed to be letters; others looked like business contracts.

There was complete silence in the cabin for some time. Finally Nelda turned around and faced the others.

Her voice was tense as she said, "These are secret papers that tell of a newly discovered diamond mine in South Africa. I judge that they have been stolen from the government offices in Johannesburg. They should not be in the hands of outsiders, especially jewel thieves!"

Everyone in the room was astonished. Each had the same question. Had these letters and documents been stolen by the same people who put the jewels in the mystery trunk, or did the girls now have another mystery to solve?

CHAPTER XV

Helpful Ad

As Nelda paused, Nancy asked, "How do you know the papers are secret?"

The girl pointed. "See the small stamp in the left-hand corner of each one? It says so."

Rod Havelock whistled. "How in the world did they get into this trunk? Obviously they're not being carried legitimately. But how does a jewel thief become involved with espionage?"

No one answered the question, but Nancy said, "I think the papers should be put into the captain's safe at once."

Everyone agreed. Rod looked at his watch. "I must go back on duty in a short time. Nancy, suppose you put the papers in a bag and we'll carry them up to Captain Detweiler's quarters."

Nancy smiled. "Good idea. And I'm glad of your protection. It's possible that spies are watching us every time we leave our cabin. If I should go alone, one of the men might pounce on me and take the papers away."

The assistant purser nodded. He waited while she found a large beach bag into which she placed the letters and agreements. Then she zipped the bag shut.

"If anyone is looking, I hope he thinks I'm going swimming," Nancy said.

Turning to the other girls, she asked them if they would put the trunk back in the wardrobe. "And lock all the doors and hide the keys," she urged.

"We'll be glad to," Nelda replied.

As soon as Nancy and Rod were gone, George locked the door of cabin one twenty-eight on the inside. Then she went back to one thirty to help the other girls.

Bess said, "What are we going to do with this soaking-wet flowered paper that Nancy and Rod took off the lid? We can't put it back yet. It won't stick."

"It certainly won't," Nelda agreed.

"Let's see if there is any room left under the bed," George suggested. "That's where we put it last time. When it's all dry, we can come back and paste it into the trunk again."

"What if it shrinks?" Bess asked.

The other girls had to admit that they had not thought of this.

Nelda said, "I have a pressing iron with me.

Do you think we dare attempt to iron the paper dry? Then it won't shrink."

George and Bess were against attempting this. Bess added, "We don't know how old it is, or what's in it. The paper might burn."

The girls decided to hide the wet paper under the bed; then they locked everything and went back to cabin one twenty-eight.

In the meantime, Nancy and Rod Havelock had been walking along the deck. In order to fully protect her, the assistant purser took her arm and kept a sharp eye out for a possible attacker. Presently they saw little Bobby run out of the lounge near them.

He stopped short, looked at the couple, then burst out, "Have-a-lock! Arm-lock! Have-a-lock! Arm-lock!"

Rod Havelock let go of Nancy's arm and dived for the little fellow, but Bobby was too quick and he ran off laughing.

Nancy knew the youngster was only teasing, but she blushed a deep red. Rod's face, too, had turned crimson. His composure was soon restored, however, and he said with a grin, "Miss Nancy Drew, may I put an armlock on you?"

The two laughed and went on to Captain Detweiler's quarters. Fortunately the officer was there. He admitted the couple at once. Then Nancy asked him to lock the door.

He smiled. "More surprises?" he asked.

She grinned back. "A big one and I think a very important one."

She unzipped the beach bag and let the papers tumble onto the captain's desk.

"I found these hidden in the lid of the mystery trunk," she said. "Nelda translated some of the documents and said they no doubt had come from the government offices in Johannesburg. I couldn't figure out why anyone stealing jewels should be involved in the espionage business at the same time."

"Perhaps he's just a contact hired to smuggle the papers into another country," the captain suggested. He picked up one document after another and quickly scanned them.

Finally he said, "These are important, indeed. Nelda and I have a relative who works for the government. He told me that some time ago a number of very important secret papers had been stolen from the office files, and there has been no trace of them. I feel sure these are the ones and will contact Johannesburg at once."

He paused for several seconds, then said, "Nancy, you have done a wonderful job of sleuthing since you've been on board, and this, perhaps, is the most important find. I think the government in Johannesburg owes you a deep debt of gratitude."

Nancy was embarrassed. She merely said, "Oh, that's high praise, but thank you. I think now I'd better leave. Please put the papers in your safe."

"Indeed, I will," the captain replied.

Nancy and Rod went outside. He said to her, "I'm due down at the purser's desk and must hurry. You don't mind if I leave you here?"

"Not at all," she responded. "And thanks a million for your help."

After breakfast the next morning Nancy wandered to the secluded area of the sports deck where she had seen Otto August twice, once alone and once with his companion.

"Maybe the two of them will be there now, talking in their finger language, and I can pick up another clue," she thought.

The girl sleuth strolled over to the spot, but no one was there. For a moment she felt a sense of disappointment, then she chided herself. "How could I expect them to be there every time I come?" Nevertheless, she walked to the men's chairs. A natural instinct for sleuthing told her to look around.

Nancy noticed a crewman picking up bits of paper and other trash that had been left near Otto August's chair. She detected a small piece of paper sticking up between two floorboards. Quickly she reached down and carefully pulled it out. To her surprise, there were three drawings on it.

They were hands showing finger language. She read: DAN.

The girl detective stared at the name for several seconds, then decided to look at the passenger list for someone named Dan or Daniel.

She hurried back to cabin one twenty-eight. The other girls were not there. Nancy scanned the passenger list, but found no one with that name. "Now what'll I do?" she asked herself. "I wonder where the girls are."

Something told her to return to the sports deck. "Perhaps I overlooked something else that was dropped," she thought.

The two suspects had not yet come to occupy their favorite chairs. Nancy went over to them and glanced around. The crewman whom she had seen cleaning up came in her direction. He was holding out a copy of *The New York Times*.

"Is this what you're looking for?" he asked. "I found it on that chair." He pointed to the one Otto August had used.

Nancy was about to turn down the offer, when her eyes focused on the date of the paper. It was one week old!

"Maybe Mr. August was reading this for a specific purpose," she told herself. "Who knows, there may even be a clue in *The New York Times!*"

She reached out to take the paper. "Thank you so much," she said, smiling at the crewman, then once more she hurried to cabin one twenty-eight. She laid the newspaper on her bed and began to look at the headlines. Most of the articles were familiar to her because she had seen them in European newspapers.

After she had turned several pages, Nancy suddenly stopped and gazed at a sheet. Something had been neatly cut out of one column!

"Mr. August must have done this!" the girl reflected. "I'll have to find out what the missing clipping said."

She decided to go to the ship's library and see if a duplicate of the newspaper was available.

The woman in charge told her, "I'm sorry, but we don't have it."

As Nancy turned away, disappointed, a passenger who had been reading nearby glanced up. "I have a copy of the *Times* of that date in my cabin," he said. "You're welcome to it. I'll get it for you."

Nancy thanked him. While he was picking it up, she looked among the books that were available to passengers. "This looks interesting," she thought. *"Life of a Waterfront Detective."*

In a few minutes the man returned with the newspaper Nancy wanted. "Here it is," he said. "I don't need it any more, so you can keep it."

"Thank you very much," Nancy replied, putting the book back. "You've been very kind."

She spread the paper on the library table and turned to the page she wanted to see. In the spot that Otto August had cut out was an advertisement. As Nancy read it, her heart began to beat faster. "What a clue!" she thought, studying the ad. A New York company desired to acquire precious flawless stones in or out of settings! "Mr. August may be already trying to find buyers for the stolen gems!" Nancy reasoned. "I wonder if that company is legitimate?"

She decided to go and tell her friends about this latest find. On her way she stopped at the purser's desk.

"What's new?" Rod asked her with a smile.

"I believe Otto August cut out an ad from *The New York Times* that was placed by a company wanting to buy precious stones," she whispered. "Here, look at this!"

The young man read the advertisement. "That figures," he said. "August is planning ahead!"

"He sure is! By the way, can you do me a favor and see if there is a crew member or an officer named Dan or Daniel? I couldn't find anyone by that name on the passenger list."

Rod thought for several seconds, then said, "I know of just one. I'll find out what I can about him."

As Nancy went off, she recalled the finger alphabet message: CREW CAN HELP FIND NECKLACE. Was Dan the crewman referred to?

She went down the stairs and walked around a corner toward her cabin. As she turned, she noticed a man in the distance standing in front of a cabin door. He seemed to either lock or unlock it. Nancy tensed. Was it cabin one twenty-eight or one thirty?

She quickened her step. The man glanced over his shoulder in her direction, then walked away in a hurry. Nancy followed, and as he turned a corner she began to run. But when she reached the cross corridor where the man had turned, no one was in sight!

"I wonder if it was August," Nancy thought and returned to her cabin. "Perhaps he was trying to get into our room again!"

She found one twenty-eight locked. She opened it and went in. No one was there, but Bess had left a note for her. It said:

Nelda, George, and I are going up to the Ping-Pong tables. George is going to play in the tournament. When you have a chance, come and join us.

But first go down and see Lou, the locksmith. He came up to the cabin and is eager to see you. He has something that will interest you very much.

Nancy folded the telltale newspaper and put it in a bureau drawer, then she locked the cabin again and hurried off to the locksmith's shop.

"You wanted to see me?" she asked the pleasant man.

"Yes, I do," Lou replied.

"Do you have another interesting lock to show me?" Nancy went on.

"No. But one of the passengers came to me with a briefcase that wouldn't open. It had a most unusual lock on it. This is what I wanted to tell you. The lock was the same kind as the one on the brass-bound trunk you asked me to open for you!"

CHAPTER XVI

Figuring Out a Capture

"WHAT a great clue!" Nancy thought upon hearing that a man had asked Lou to open a briefcase that had the same type of lock as the one on the mystery trunk!

She asked the locksmith, "What was the passenger's name?"

"I don't know," Lou said, shaking his head. "He didn't tell me."

Nancy was crestfallen. She had come so close to making a great discovery!

Lou must have noticed her disappointment. He smiled. "But I did see two initials inside the briefcase. They were O.A."

Nancy felt like exclaiming over this exciting bit of evidence, but she said nothing. The girl detective thought, "Those are the initials of Otto August!"

She asked Lou, "What did the man look like?"

The locksmith gave a description that in no way matched that of Otto August. It did, however, fit his companion perfectly!

She assumed that August had asked his friend to take the briefcase to Lou so he could not be traced. She smiled. "Even a thief can make a mistake," she thought. "He forgot about his initials."

The girl detective asked Lou what the man who had brought the briefcase had talked about while he was there. She expected the reply to be about locks and keys. But she was wrong.

"Besides asking for a new key, the man talked about the weather and the speed of the *Winschoten*. You know, Miss Drew, that we dock in New York the day after tomorrow!"

"I'd forgotten about that. Time has flown," Nancy admitted. To herself she said, "I'd better get this mystery solved in a hurry." She thanked Lou and left his shop.

Before lunch Nancy went back to the purser's desk. Rod was on duty and not particularly busy, so she could confide her latest findings to him without being overheard.

The young man shook his head. "You are something, Nancy Drew!"

The girl told him that she had had another hunch and would like to visit the hold again. "When you're off duty, Rod, would you take me down there?"

"I'll be glad to," Rod replied and grinned. "The man who takes my place at the counter for the next shift will be here in five minutes. Can you wait that long?"

"I won't move," Nancy replied.

The replacement officer arrived on time, and Nancy and Rod set off.

On the way she asked, "Would you please ask Pieter if anyone has ever inquired about the trunk with the initials N.D. on it?"

"Sure," Rod replied.

After going down the narrow iron stairway and past the boiler room, the couple finally came to the door of the hold. Nancy rang the bell. No answer. Rod pushed the button again.

It was several minutes before the door was opened. Pieter stood there. "Hello," he said with a friendly grin.

"Hi, Pieter," Havelock said. "I'm glad to see you're well again." Then he proceeded to speak to him in his native language. Nancy, of course, could not understand a word.

Pieter replied in the same language. Finally Rod turned to Nancy and said, "He says that to his knowledge no one has ever inquired about the mystery trunk."

"I wish I knew what Otto August was thinking," Nancy said. "Does he believe his trunk is in the hold? He knows it's not in our cabin, because I'm sure he was the one who ransacked it."

"I'm inclined to believe that August must be convinced it was taken to the hold," Rod said. "He doesn't know about the empty room next to yours."

"Perhaps we should take the trunk into the hold late tonight," Nancy suggested. "Then it will be unloaded with the other baggage and he'll claim it when we arrive. If he should see it being carried out of our cabin, though, he might be afraid we found his jewels!"

Rod asked her if she had examined it any further. "Or are you satisfied that you've taken out everything that was hidden inside?"

Nancy said that she had thoroughly felt all the other parts of the trunk. "I'm positive there's nothing else in it," she told him.

"I'll be off duty this evening," Rod said. "Suppose we make a date for two A.M. to carry it down to the hold."

"I'll be ready," Nancy said. "See you then."

"By the way," Rod said, "I asked about the crewman named Dan. He has a fine reputation and in no way could be connected with your mystery of stolen jewels."

Nancy nodded. "Thanks for checking. I wonder whom Otto August was referring to."

Before returning to her cabin, the young sleuth decided to see Captain Detweiler and tell him about the latest developments. Fortunately, the officer was in his quarters and welcomed his caller.

"More news?" he asked.

"Perhaps," Nancy replied and told him everything she had learned since last talking to him.

The captain remarked, "There's an old saying about a person who doesn't let any grass grow under his feet. I'd apply this to you, except there isn't a blade of grass on this ship!"

Nancy laughed. "What I came to ask you," she said, "is about having August arrested when we arrive in New York. If you have not already done so, would you mind asking the authorities to be sure that customs men are alerted and waiting on the pier in the section where the two N.D. trunks will be placed."

"I certainly will," the captain replied.

"You might tell them that the gang of jewel thieves uses the finger language to communicate," Nancy went on. "One of their buddies might be on the pier to meet and signal them. In that case, he should be arrested, too."

The captain nodded.

"I'll ask Bess and George to follow August," Nancy went on. "Nelda and I plan to be the first ones off the ship so that we can be at the place where his trunk will be put."

Captain Detweiler thought her whole plan was good. "You certainly worked this out well, Nancy.

I will also inform them that the State Department should be called in on this with reference to the stolen documents."

"Did you talk to the government in Johannesburg about that yet?" Nancy inquired.

"Indeed, I did," the captain replied. "The papers were stolen some time ago, and the government suspects an official in the commerce department. However, so far they have not been able to gather enough evidence against him. You have given them their best clue yet!"

"I have?" Nancy asked. "How?"

"The suspect's name is Hans August!"

"Wow! You mean he's related to Otto?"

"Johannesburg ran a check on him and they found he's Otto's brother. They suspect Hans works with an underground group in New York that is extremely interested in these papers. Since his brother is evidently an accomplished smuggler, he must have given Otto the papers to transport secretly to the United States."

Nancy was elated. "So we might have accidentally uncovered an industrial espionage ring of international dimensions?"

"That's right. As long as Otto August goes ahead and claims his trunk, we can nail him and his brother, too!"

"There's one more person who should be arrested," Nancy went on. "Remember the woman who we believe planted the diamond bracelet on Nelda in Johannesburg?"

"Yes. Evidently she's August's wife. I found out he is married."

Nancy finally got back to her cabin just as the other girls were arriving.

They were amazed about the documents and the espionage ring. Nelda marveled at how Nancy was drawing the net closer around the suspected jewel robber and his brother. "Perhaps August will admit that the bracelet was planted on me," she said hopefully. "This way I would be vindicated. Oh, Nancy, you all have been so wonderful to me!"

George, who did not like obvious compliments, immediately changed the subject. "Isn't anyone hungry except me?" she asked. "I could eat three lunches right now."

Bess giggled. "I'm with you."

"Then let's go," George urged. "I hope they have roast beef sandwiches on the menu."

Later that afternoon Nancy and Nelda went to one of the lower decks to listen to an orchestra concert in one of the lounges. They were standing outside, peering through a window and oblivious to what was going on behind them. They did not notice that Bobby was whizzing toward them on a skateboard.

The little fellow seemed to be manipulating his

plaything very well. As he neared the girls, however, he deliberately turned and ran into both of them!

Nancy and Nelda were knocked off their feet, and sat down hard on the deck. They looked around to see what had hit them. Bobby stood off at a distance, grinning and holding his skateboard in one hand.

"You bad boy!" Nelda scolded angrily. "If you can't use that thing properly, you shouldn't be racing around the deck on it!"

"I'm sorry I knocked you over," Bobby said contritely. "I only meant to hit you a little bit. Real easy like."

By this time the two girls were on their feet and looking hard at the boy.

Nancy said, "Bobby, there is a big difference between playing a joke and doing something that hurts people."

Bobby hung his head. "I said I was sorry."

"That's not enough!" Nancy replied. "I want to know why you did it."

For a few seconds Bobby did not answer. He looked a bit frightened, but finally said, "Those funny men made me do it!"

"What funny men?"

"Oh, you know, those two guys that do silly things with their fingers."

Nancy was startled. She wondered if the little boy meant Otto August and his companion. She put up her own right hand and began to spell out her name. "Like this?" she asked.

Bobby looked amazed. "You know how to do that, too?"

"Yes," she answered, "but I don't know the whole alphabet. This is the kind of sign language deaf people use to talk to one another."

Nancy now quizzed the boy about the two men who had urged him to run into the girls.

"Who were they, Bobby?" she asked.

"I don't know," Bobby replied and ran off.

CHAPTER XVII

Overboard!

Bobby fled down the hall. Nancy hesitated, then said to Nelda, "I think we should make him identify the men and go talk to them."

Nelda agreed, and the two girls sped off in the direction the little boy had taken. It was not hard to locate Bobby and tell him what they wanted him to do.

At first he refused to go. "The men might hurt me and think I'm a tattletale!" he cried out, hanging back.

Nancy said she and Nelda were sure they knew who the men were. Bobby need not talk to them if he did not wish to do so. All he had to do was identify them. Finally he agreed to go along.

On a hunch, Nancy headed for the secluded corner of the top deck. Her guess had been right. Otto August and his companion were seated there. At the moment they were not talking or using the finger language.

"Bobby, are they the two men?" Nelda asked.

The little boy nodded. "I didn't tell you something else about them. They gave me a quarter to run into you."

Nelda frowned. "That sounds like them. It was a mean thing to do."

She, Nancy, and Bobby walked up to the men. Nancy spoke first. "We want to know why you put this little boy up to running into us on his skateboard!" she demanded.

Nelda added at once, "He hit us so hard that he knocked us down. We might have been badly hurt."

Otto August looked at Bobby and said, "Why did you do that?"

The boy answered promptly, "Because you told me to and paid me to do it."

"I never told you to hurt the girls, just to tease them," Otto August went on, glaring at the small boy angrily.

Bobby looked a little frightened, but said, "You didn't say anything about teasing. You told me to run into them!"

Otto August turned to Nancy and Nelda. "I hope you don't believe what he's been telling you. My friend and I were trying to have a private conversation, but couldn't because this child came up and kept talking and talking. We wanted to get rid of him, so all I said was, 'Why don't you go find Nancy Drew and her friends and tease them?'"

Bobby's eyes flashed. "You did not! You never said anything like that! You told me to run into them!"

"That's not true!" Otto August shouted. "You are a wicked little liar!"

The girls were amazed at Bobby's defiance. Instead of being frightened any longer, he was defending himself very well. He looked at the two men in disgust. "You know what you are?" he asked. "You're just like the bad men on TV!"

Mr. August blinked at this accusation but flared back, "And you know what I think about you? You're a fresh little kid who talks entirely too much!"

The two men rose from their chairs and hurried off. Nancy and Nelda were puzzled.

"Who was telling the truth, August or Bobby?" Nelda asked.

The girls were inclined to believe the boy was.

"Can I go now?" Bobby wanted to know.

"Okay," Nancy said. "But don't hurt anyone else with your skateboard!"

"I won't," Bobby called back over his shoulder as he ran off.

Nancy and Nelda returned to their cabin. Bess and George were there and reminded the girls that this was to be the night of the captain's dinner.

"Is anybody going in costume?" Bess asked. "You know the notice said that you could come in costume if you wished."

George grinned. "Can you imagine eating dinner with a mask on?"

Nancy felt that the masquerade they had already had was enough for her. All the girls decided to wear long evening dresses. When they walked into the dining room, each found a note at her place.

"Oh!" Nelda exclaimed. "An invitation to a date!"

"Really?" George picked up hers. "What does it say?"

"I'm to meet Al on the top deck at nine o'clock," Nancy announced.

"Chipper wants me to come up at nine-ten," Nelda said.

"And Bruce says nine-twenty!" Bess said.

"They must be playing a joke on us," George decided. "I'm supposed to see Tubby at nine-thirty!"

"I wonder what the boys have in mind," Bess said with a giggle. "Maybe a surprise!"

After a delicious dinner, Nelda said, "Nancy, since your time and mine aren't far apart, why don't we go up together?"

"You might spoil the boys' surprise," George suggested.

Nancy thought it would be a good idea for the girls to go in twos. "I don't like the sound of this. The whole thing is a little strange. Suppose the invitations aren't from the boys but are a trap?"

George laughed. "Nancy, you're getting overcautious. Of course the notes are from the boys. As a matter of fact, I heard Chipper mention something about dates after nine tonight."

"Well, that makes me feel better," Nancy admitted. "But I'd rather go with Nelda anyway."

When the girls arrived at the top deck, no one was in sight. Soon two figures appeared, however, and walked up to them. They were dressed as fishermen and wore stocking masks. They gesticulated in a funny way and made little dancing steps in between. The girls laughed. Which of the boys had thought up this clever disguise?

When the fishermen reached the girls, they both made a little bow. Then they each grabbed a girl and picked her up.

Only when the fishermen pushed them close to the railing did Nancy and Nelda realize that these people were not their friends, and that they intended to throw both girls overboard!

"Oh, they mustn't!" Nancy thought desperately and mustered up every ounce of strength to fight off her attackers.

She and Nelda struggled frantically, but they were no match for their strong enemies. The men had a good grip on them, and seconds later they went over, their screams drowned out by the waves!

In the dining room a few minutes before, Al and his three friends stopped at the table where Bess and George were still sitting.

Nancy and Nelda were no match for their enemies.

"We were finished eating early, so we thought we might as well pick you up here," Al said. "Where are Nancy and Nelda?"

"They went up to the top deck," Bess replied. "You left these notes here saying you wanted to meet us there ten minutes apart, but Nancy and Nelda went together. Why did you stagger the times of our dates?"

"What are you talking about?" Al looked puzzled. "We put nine forty-five on all our invitations!"

George stared at him. "Something's wrong! Let's look at the notes again and try to figure this out!"

The young people studied the writing. "It's been altered!" Chipper blurted out. "The times have been changed."

"We'd better get up to the deck quickly," George said. "Come on, everybody!"

The six young people raced up the stairs. They had just reached the top deck when they heard Nancy and Nelda cry out for help as they were tossed overboard. The two fishermen sped away and were lost to view within seconds.

Bess screamed. Al ran to the railing, saying he would jump in after the girls. George grabbed his arm and held him back.

"You'll never find them and would probably drown yourself!" she exclaimed. "We must notify the captain at once!"

While Bess stood there, paralyzed with fright, George ran to a wall phone and picked it up. As soon as a man's voice answered, she cried out, "Stop the ship at once! Two girls were thrown overboard. Quick! Do something!"

"Just a minute," the man said. "Stay on the line." He gave orders through his intercom, then spoke to Bess again. "Who are the girls?"

"Nancy Drew and Nelda Detweiler," George replied. She was shaking by now. "Please, don't let them drown!"

"We're holding the ship," the man told her in a reassuring voice. "Don't worry. Just stay by the phone for a moment. The captain might want to talk to you."

Within seconds, the great ocean liner slowed and finally came to a stop. Then the wall phone rang and George picked it up. Captain Detweiler was calling. "Who is this speaking?" he asked.

"George Fayne. Nancy and Nelda were just thrown overboard by two masked men dressed as fishermen, but they disappeared."

"Which side of the ship are the girls on?" the captain asked quickly, trying to keep his voice steady and calm.

"Starboard," George replied.

"We'll lower a rescue launch at once," the captain promised and hung up.

George joined the five young people who stood at the rail and watched. A motor launch was let down from the deck to the water, and a great searchlight on it beamed ahead as the boat set off toward the rear of the ship.

Meanwhile, Nancy and Nelda, expert swimmers, had twisted their bodies and dived correctly into the ocean. They had come to the surface unhurt, and had begun to swim in the direction of the *Winschoten*. However, they soon realized it was too far away already for them to reach it, and their strength was giving out.

Horrible thoughts raced through Nancy's mind. A shark might be on the prowl! A floating log might ram into her and Nelda! Perhaps no one noticed that they were missing and they would be left to drown!

"I mustn't lose my nerve," Nancy thought. "It would be best if Nelda and I stick together, and maybe we'll be rescued."

She shouted the girl's name several times, but there was no answer. Nancy's heart sank. Had something happened to Nelda?

CHAPTER XVIII

Telltale Shoes

NELDA swam furiously toward the *Winschoten*. Every few moments she would pause and shout Nancy's name, but she received no response.

The girls were not within hearing distance, and their shouts were drowned out by the roaring waves. Each hoped fervently that the other was all right. Both were shaking with cold and fear. Suddenly their hopes were revived. The ocean liner had stopped! Someone had missed them after all!

In another minute, they spotted the strong searchlight of the oncoming launch. It was headed in their direction! Both girls managed to hold up their right and left arms alternately while staying afloat, so that they might be seen. The move was enough to signal their rescuers.

First the launch stopped to pick up Nelda, who was a little closer. A crewman dropped a rope ladder over the side and the weary swimmer grabbed it. As she climbed up helpful arms extended to her and pulled her into the launch.

"Are you all right?" a young officer asked anxiously as Nelda dropped onto the floor of the small vessel.

"Yes," Nelda gasped. "Yes, I'm fine. But I don't know about Nancy. Please find her!"

"Don't worry, we saw her waving her arm. She'll be okay," the young man assured Nelda, and he covered the shivering girl with a blanket. "Just relax and rest for a few moments."

A minute later the launch spotted Nancy and soon she, too, had been hauled aboard. The young officer asked her if she felt okay.

Nancy smiled wanly as she replied, "Yes, but I never want to have another experience like that again!"

After Nancy had been wrapped in a blanket and the launch was headed back toward the *Winschoten,* the officer asked the girls, "Now tell me, how did you happen to fall overboard?"

"Fall!" Nancy cried out indignantly. "We were thrown into the ocean by two masked men!"

"What!" The officer was thunderstruck. "But who would do a thing like that?"

"Well," Nancy said, "it's a long story but we have mysterious enemies on board. We suspect they're international jewel thieves who are afraid we'll expose them."

"Did you recognize the men?" the officer asked.

"No. That's just it. They wore fishermen's suits and stocking masks," Nancy said. "We can't identify them because of their disguises."

By this time the launch was alongside the ocean liner. Each girl was put into a rescue chair and pulled aboard. There were hundreds of onlookers staring down from the various decks. Nancy and Nelda ignored all the questions that were shouted at them, and only waved briefly to their friends to let them know they were feeling all right.

Bess, George, and the four boys followed the girls, who were taken to the infirmary. While their friends waited outside, Nancy and Nelda were examined by Dr. Karl.

He could not find anything seriously wrong with them. "You're pretty hardy girls," he said when he had finished. "I'm just glad the water wasn't very cold. I recommend hot baths, and then to bed. Better stay here overnight and get a good rest."

The girls did not object, and two nurses took charge of them. After they were tucked into beds, side by side, Captain Detweiler visited. He was very upset.

"Too many strange things have happened on this trip," he said. "But this last incident is atrocious. I have instituted a thorough search for the two phony fishermen."

After the captain had gone, Nelda fell asleep, but Nancy lay awake. She felt all right and wanted to get up to continue her sleuthing. It had suddenly occurred to her that perhaps she had a clue to one of the fishermen.

"Anyway, I have a two A.M. date with Rod to carry the mystery trunk to the hold," she reasoned. When a nurse came in, she asked to see Dr. Karl. He came at once and she told him she felt perfectly well.

"Please," she said, "let my friends bring me some dry clothes. I want to go back to my own cabin."

The physician smiled and said, "I'm sure that'll be all right. But you'll have to promise me that you'll take it easy!"

Nancy laughed. "I'll promise. One midsummer night's swim was enough for me!"

Nancy phoned Bess and George, who had gone to their cabin after being told that the girls would stay in the infirmary overnight. She asked them to bring dry clothes for her.

"You're going to get up?" Bess asked.

"Yes," Nancy replied.

By this time Nelda had awakened, and when she realized Nancy was leaving, she indicated that she wanted to go, too. "Tell Bess to bring some things for me, too," she said to Nancy.

Bess and George arrived in a short time with fresh clothes for the two girls, and Dr. Karl released them both. They returned to cabin one twenty-eight and sat down.

"One reason why I wanted to come back here,"

Nancy explained to her friends, "is that I have a slight clue to one of the fake fishermen. He was wearing a pair of very unusual shoes. They were like Dutch wooden shoes, but made of leather."

Nelda was astounded to hear this. "I didn't even notice what my attacker had on his feet," she said.

George asked, "How are you going to find out who owns them?"

"I'm not sure. Maybe Rod can help."

Nancy called Havelock's number. Rod promised to come right down to their cabin.

"You girls have made a lightning recovery," he said when he arrived. "You're amazing."

Nancy told Rod she wanted him to help her hunt for a pair of shoes, and described them.

"I'll ask each steward if he has seen such a pair in any of the passengers' cabins," Rod offered, and got on the telephone. He could not reach all the men and left messages for them to call him at cabin one twenty-eight.

It seemed a long time to the girls, and the answer from each steward was negative. None of them had seen such an odd pair of shoes in any of the cabins they serviced.

Rod Havelock, too, was disappointed. Instead of leaving he stood in the middle of the room, looking up into space. Finally he said, "I just thought of something. It seems to me that one of the crewmen has such a pair of shoes."

"Can we go and ask him now?" Nancy urged.

"Yes. Let's do that."

Again Nancy recalled the finger language message in which the word *crew* had appeared.

When the two reached the crew's quarters, Rod knocked on the door of the man he had in mind. The fellow opened and asked in Dutch what Havelock wanted.

Rod replied in the same language, so Nancy had to wait for a translation. She was amazed and delighted when the crewman brought out a pair of shoes just like the ones she had seen on the phony fisherman!

She wanted to ask questions, but knowing that the man could not understand her, she remained silent.

Havelock listened carefully to the fellow's explanation, then he translated for Nancy. "A passenger borrowed his shoes for the costume party. This man here set them outside his door and the passenger picked them up."

"Who was the passenger?"

"He says he can't identify him because he never saw him. The borrower had shoved a printed note under his door and requested that the crewman leave the shoes outside. Later the shoes were returned with several *guilders* in them."

Nancy was disappointed and asked if the man still had the printed note. Unfortunately, he had thrown it away.

Havelock thanked the man for the information, then he and Nancy walked back upstairs. For several minutes not a word was spoken between them. Finally Nancy remarked, "Those evil men are clever."

"Yes," Rod replied. "Too bad we didn't catch them in the act."

He left her at the door of one twenty-eight, saying, "I'll be back for you at two A.M. In the meantime, you'd better catch a little sleep. You've had a harrowing evening."

Nancy had every intention of following his advice, but when she stepped inside her room she found the other girls waiting for her. They wanted to talk.

"Did you have any luck?" George asked.

The young detective shook her head. "Not much," she said and told them what the crewman had said.

"This is so frustrating!" Bess said. "Too bad we don't have any hard evidence."

"Couldn't the captain arrest August for smuggling the jewels and documents?" Nelda asked.

"He can't be accused of smuggling the jewels yet. Only when he goes through customs without declaring them," Nancy said. "I don't know about the documents, but he might be able to talk his way out of that one. He could say it's not his trunk!"

Nancy decided not to undress, but the other girls did and got into bed. They found, however, that they could not sleep.

Suddenly Nancy thought of something. "You

know," she said, "we forgot to put the paper back into the trunk!"

"We'd better do it now," George said. "Come on, girls, put on your robes and slippers."

They jumped out of bed and a few minutes later followed Nancy into cabin one thirty. Once more the strange trunk was taken from the wardrobe, set on the floor, and opened. After they had emptied the piece of luggage, Nancy said, "I really didn't examine the sides as thoroughly as the bottom and the lid. Before we put the paper back in, let me check this out."

She ran her fingers all along the sides. When she came to one corner, she said, "The paper seems to come off here very easily!"

"Why not remove it and see what's underneath?" George suggested.

Nancy did just that, and the girls stared at what she uncovered. It was a purple velvet cloth, and part of a diamond was sticking out through a small slit in it!

Carefully Nancy lifted the velvet cloth. The girls were speechless at what they saw. Below the covering was a second matching cloth. To this had been sewn rings, pins, bracelets, and tiny velvet bags containing precious jewels!

Bess sighed in awe. "Oh, these are beautiful! It's a good thing we didn't miss them!"

Nelda ran her fingers over the stones. "I can't believe it! I just can't believe it!"

Nancy spoke up. "Nelda, the bracelet you were accused of stealing—is it here?"

Nelda shook her head sadly. "No."

"Don't you think we should call the captain?" George suggested. "Let's ask him to come down immediately. These jewels have to be put into his safe before the trunk goes into the hold."

"You're right," Nancy agreed.

George went into the adjoining cabin and dialed the captain's number.

"Yes?" he said.

Quickly George explained that it was imperative for him to come down to his niece's cabin at once.

"Is she ill?" he asked, worried.

"No, she's fine," George replied. "There's another reason. I can't tell you on the phone."

"I'll be there in a few minutes," Captain Detweiler promised.

The girls removed the piece with the precious stones from the trunk, but put the purple cover back in place.

"It's going to be a hard job putting this paper back over the velvet," Bess remarked.

Nancy nodded. "To tell you the truth," she said, "I think it's impossible."

"Suppose August opens the trunk and sees what we've done. He could say he made a mistake and it isn't his," Bess said.

"He has to unlock it first," George said. "And

by doing that he proves it's his because he has the keys!"

"Good thinking," Nancy agreed. "Let's forget about the paper. As a matter of fact, let's rip it all out, just to make sure we didn't miss anything."

This was quickly done, but nothing more was found underneath the paper on the opposite side. The girls locked the trunk again and put it back into the wardrobe.

At this moment there was a knock on the door of cabin one twenty-eight. Quickly they hurried into their room and walked up to the door together. If the person who had knocked was not the captain, they would be prepared!

CHAPTER XIX

A Tense Wait

To the relief of Nancy and the other girls, the caller was Captain Detweiler. They showed him the new cache of jewelry and he looked grim.

"In all my voyages back and forth across the ocean," he said, "I have never encountered a mystery as outrageous as this one!"

He found that the long velvet pad with the jewels sewed to it would not fit into his pocket. "I'll have to carry this treasure some other way."

Nancy said, "How about asking Rod to bring one of your empty safe-deposit cases from the purser's office?"

"I'll do that," the captain replied.

He went back to cabin one twenty-eight and called the assistant purser. Havelock said he would come down as quickly as possible and bring an empty case with him. He arrived a few minutes

later and gazed at the new find with disbelief.
Then he grinned and looked at Nancy.

"I thought you were going to bed and get some
sleep before two A.M. Here you are, still working
on the mystery!"

The girl detective smiled back. "I never would
have forgiven myself if I hadn't finished investi-
gating the trunk and had later learned that we
missed all these jewels!"

The priceless piece of velvet with its contents
was put into the small case, then Nancy brought
out a brown beach towel to wrap around it.

"This way no one will know what you're carrying," she reasoned, "in case you meet a passenger
or a crew member on the way back."

"Good idea," Rod Havelock said. "Besides, if
the captain and I are attacked again, this case is a
beautiful weapon for our defense. I wouldn't like
to be hit on the head with sharp metal this
heavy!"

After the two men had left, Nancy glanced at
her watch. There was very little time left before
two A.M., but she slept long enough to feel re-
freshed.

Rod picked her up at the appointed time, and
the two carried the trunk out into the corridor.
No one was in sight, and Rod told her that the
watchman was at the far end of the ship.

Nancy whispered, "The trunk seems lighter
than it did before."

"It is," Rod said, "and for a good reason!"

By the time Nancy and Rod had reached the hold, however, their arms were weary from their burden. Rod unlocked the door and they carried the trunk inside.

"Am I glad that we've got it down here safely," Nancy said with a sigh of relief.

"So am I," the assistant purser remarked. "Come on, let's get back upstairs. You must go to bed. No one can get along with as little sleep as you've been getting lately."

He escorted her to her cabin, said good night, and told her not to worry about anything. Then he whispered, "I've enjoyed working with you. In my opinion you're one of the cleverest sleuths in the world. I'll miss playing detective with you, Nancy."

The girl smiled and whispered back, "If I ever travel on the *Winschoten* again, I'll see if I can dig up a good mystery for you to solve with me."

She went into her cabin, undressed quickly, and fell asleep at once. She was awakened at seven o'clock by the other girls. They were whispering and giggling.

"What's so funny?" Nancy asked, rubbing her eyes.

George replied, "I was just telling Bess and Nelda that I dreamed someone stole my shoes and left me wooden ones with turned-up toes instead."

Nancy chuckled and hurried to dress. Before

the girls were ready to leave their cabin, the phone rang. Nancy picked it up. The caller was Al.

"Do you girls feel all right after your swim last night?" he asked.

"Oh just fine, Al. Thank you," Nancy replied.

"I'm terribly sorry I couldn't jump into the water and save you," the boy went on. "You girls are great divers and swimmers."

Nancy laughed. "Knowing how came in handy. Have you eaten yet?"

"No," Al replied. "Why don't we all have a farewell breakfast together?"

The girls accepted and in a few minutes went to the dining room, where they met the boys. When they had finished eating, they all said they hoped they could have a reunion some time.

Then Nancy and her friends returned to their cabin. The phone rang again and Nancy answered the call.

"Hello!" said a familiar voice.

"Ned!" she almost shouted. "Oh, it's wonderful to hear from you."

Ned told her that Burt Eddleton and Dave Evans, George's and Bess's friends, were with him. "We're driving to New York to pick you up," Ned said.

"That's great!" Nancy replied. "I'll be glad to have a ride all the way home. But Ned, your car isn't big enough for three extra passengers, a brass-bound trunk and several bags and suit-cases!"

Ned laughed. "My Dad recently bought a new station wagon, and we're using that."

He went on to say that he and his companions would meet the girls as close to the entrance of the pier as visitors were allowed to come.

Burt and Dave spoke to George and Bess, kidding them about taking a leisurely luxury cruise while the boys were working, then they all said good-by.

At once Nancy and the other girls began to pack. There was silence for several minutes, but suddenly Nelda cried out.

"What's the matter?" Bess asked, startled by the exclamation.

Nelda said that the bracelet she had been wearing the night she went overboard was missing. "I know I had it on when I went to the infirmary," she said. "After that I don't remember."

"Oh, dear, I hope you haven't lost it," Bess told her.

"So do I. My dear grandmother gave it to me and I prized it highly because she's no longer living."

George asked, "Was it terribly valuable?"

"No," Nelda replied, "but I loved it for sentimental reasons."

George suggested that Nelda call the infirmary and ask if the bracelet had been found there.

Nelda did, but was told no one had come across it. Disappointed, she heaved a great sigh. "I guess it's gone forever!"

Just then there was a knock on the door. Nancy opened it to find Heinrich standing outside.

"Did any of you lose a piece of jewelry?" he asked.

"Yes, I did," Nelda answered quickly. "A bracelet."

"What did it look like?" the steward inquired.

"It was a string of tiny enamel flowers in various colors."

Heinrich put a hand into a side pocket and pulled out a bracelet. "Is this it?"

"Oh, yes, it is!" Nelda replied, delighted. "Where did you find it?"

Heinrich said that after he had tidied the various cabins, he was putting all the soiled linen into a bundle when the bracelet fell out.

He smiled. "I figured it probably belonged to one of you."

Nelda thanked him and he hurried off. When she had closed the door, she said, "I'm ashamed to think that I was ever suspicious of Heinrich. I'm sure this proves his complete innocence of any involvement with the mystery trunk."

"You're right," George said, and Nancy and Bess agreed.

Late that afternoon all the luggage except a

small quantity, which the girls would carry, was put in the corridor to be picked up later and placed near the large opening of the ship that led directly to the pier.

That evening the girls said good-by to all their new acquaintances on shipboard, and went to bed early. They wanted to be up with the sunrise, since Nancy and Nelda had decided they wanted to be the first passengers off the ship.

"I think I won't even bother with breakfast," Nancy said when they woke the next morning. "Nelda, let's eat some of last night's fruit and the rest of the crackers in this box."

It did not take them long to finish the skimpy meal. Then they checked once more with Bess and George on where they would be standing.

"Near the inside door leading to the gangplank," George said. "When we see Otto August and his companion file out, we're to fall right behind."

"Exactly," said Nancy. "And give me a signal."

She and Nelda picked up their purses and hand luggage and left the cabin. Not many people were in the corridors yet, so the girls made good time to the exit where the gangplank would be set up. They had no trouble finding a place at the head of what could be a long line of debarking passengers.

The *Winschoten* was already at the pier, but

the exit door had not yet been opened. Through a window Nancy and Nelda could see baggage being taken from the hold out onto the dock.

"There goes the N.D. trunk," Nancy whispered.

Finally the exit door to the gangplank was opened. A group of officers marched off the ship first and presented papers to authorities on the pier.

Rod Havelock was among them. He paused for a fraction of a second and whispered to the girls, "Good luck!"

To Nancy and Nelda it seemed as if their wait was interminable. At last, however, the signal was given for passengers to start debarking. Excited, the girls hurried down the gangplank and onto the pier. They were met by two men.

One of them opened his coat and showed a card. He was from the FBI! "Are you Nancy Drew and Nelda Detweiler?" he asked.

"Yes," Nancy answered.

"I'm Mr. Carson and this is my assistant. We want to question you about a theft!"

CHAPTER XX

The Trap

NANCY and Nelda were nonplussed by the request of the FBI agents. "Wh-what do you mean?" Nelda asked. "Why do you want to question us?"

"There is no charge and we're not arresting you," replied Mr. Carson. "But the Dutch police have informed us that they have reason to believe that you, Nelda Detweiler, smuggled a diamond bracelet into Holland and sold it there with the help of Nancy Drew!"

"But that's ridiculous," Nancy put in. "Nelda and I didn't even meet until we were aboard ship!"

"Miss Detweiler," the FBI man went on, ignoring Nancy's outburst, "didn't you get in trouble with a jewelry store in Johannesburg?"

"I was falsely accused of stealing a diamond bracelet. But it was straightened out before I left," Nelda was close to tears.

Nancy put an arm around the distressed girl, and said to Mr. Carson, "This is a dreadful mistake, and I think I know who's behind it!"

"Suppose you tell me your side of the story," Carson said.

"Nelda and I met on board the *Winschoten* and shared a cabin with two other friends of mine," Nancy began. "A trunk was delivered to us with the initials N.D. on it, but it belonged neither to Nelda nor me. Since it had no tags, the captain and we opened it, trying to find out which passenger it belonged to."

"And did you?"

"No, there were no clues. But meanwhile we have a strong suspicion. Also, we found lots of gems and diamond jewelry hidden cleverly in concealed compartments of the trunk. They're now in the captain's safe."

The FBI men looked at each other. "Well, that's interesting news," Carson said. "I suppose the captain notified customs authorities here in New York?"

"Yes, he did," Nancy continued. "And the state department. There were stolen secret papers in the trunk too."

"What secret papers?"

"Reports on a new diamond mine that was found in South Africa," Nelda explained.

The FBI man whistled. "You made quite a discovery! Go ahead with your story, please."

"There are two men on board," Nancy went on, "who have been after the mystery trunk ever since we left Rotterdam. They did not claim it officially, probably because they were afraid. They used the finger alphabet to communicate with each other, obviously because they wanted to make sure they wouldn't be overheard. One is named Otto August, but I don't know the name of the other man."

"Are they still aboard?" Carson's assistant questioned.

"Yes. My two friends who shared our cabin are watching them."

Nelda said, "It must have been Otto August or one of his confederates who tried to get Nancy and me in trouble with the FBI."

"Of course," Nancy agreed. She told the agents about the man who saw Otto August off in Rotterdam and signaled to him in finger language to beware of Nancy Drew and NE.

"He probably informed the Dutch government of this trumped-up charge to get us out of the way, so August could claim his trunk without interference from us."

"Of course he didn't know that we had already found all the jewels and papers," Nelda added.

"I believe you're telling the truth," Mr. Carson said. "But you understand that we'll have to stay with you until your story is proved."

"I don't think you'll have to wait long," Nancy

said. "If you'll come with me, I'll show you where the mystery trunk is.

She led the men toward the unloading dock. After some searching, she found the strange trunk in the D section.

"There it is," she pointed. "And mine is over here. You see how much alike they are?"

"You're right," Carson admitted.

"August is coming down the gangplank," Nelda said. "Bess and George are right behind him."

"I think he should not see you two girls until he has claimed his trunk," Mr. Carson said. "We won't be able to nab him without proof, and he might be afraid to go ahead if you're here. Come on, let's get behind that pillar over there. Quick!"

He pulled the girls with him, and his assistant followed. From their hiding place they observed Otto August and his friend reach the end of the gangplank and glance around the pier. Then they walked directly to the D section.

"This is my trunk," August announced to the customs inspector, laying his hand on the unmarked piece.

"Do you have a claim check?" the customs man asked.

"Of course," August said and produced the ticket.

"But this trunk has no identification," the man objected.

"I have the key for it. Here. I'll prove it to

you." August produced the key and unlocked the trunk.

"Okay," the man said. "What are you declaring?"

"Nothing. All I have in there are old costumes. I sometimes do amateur acting."

At this moment Nancy, Nelda, and the two FBI men walked up. Bess and George also arrived at the scene.

"Good morning, Mr. August," Nancy said.

The suspect looked startled, but returned the greeting. Then he said to the customs official, "The initials on the trunk are my wife's. It's an old one and she never bothered to have them changed."

"Is she with you?"

"No, I'm traveling alone."

"What is your name, sir?"

"Otto August."

"Mr. August, would you please open your trunk?"

The man produced the key again and did as he was told. When he threw back the lid he gasped. "Someone has been in here!" he screamed. "All the lining has been torn off!"

"We know, Mr. August," the customs man said evenly. "We also know what you had hidden in there. You're under arrest for trying to smuggle diamonds and other jewels and stolen government papers into the United States!"

August paled, and his friend, who had been standing behind him, tried to sneak away unobtrusively. But the customs officials arrested him as an accomplice and snapped handcuffs on both men before they had a chance to escape.

"This is ridiculous," August exploded. "If there were smugglers on board, you should have investigated them. I have nothing incriminating in my trunk, and you can't pin this rap on me!"

The customs official paid no attention to his outburst. He proceeded to remove the clothes from the trunk. First came a pair of overalls with paint spots on them. He was about to lay them aside, when something caught his attention. He reached into the pocket and pulled out a wig and a black curly beard.

"Wait a minute!" Nelda cried out. She stared at the beard, then at Otto August. "Would you please put this disguise on the suspect?" she asked the customs man.

He held the beard against August's face while Nancy slipped the wig on his head. The infuriated prisoner tried to prevent them from doing it, but without success.

"Now I recognize him!" Nelda exclaimed. "He's the thief who stole the diamonds from the jewelry shop in Johannesburg. Oh, Nancy, all this time he was right on board the *Winschoten* with us!"

"And he didn't know whether you recognized

him or not," Nancy added. "That's why he didn't claim his trunk. He saw it brought into our cabin, and noticed you standing there when he looked in the open door. So he complained to the porter, and when the porter asked August to identify his piece, the suspect disappeared because he would have to do it in your presence!"

"Did you find the bracelet you were accused of stealing in this trunk, Miss Detweiler?" the FBI man Carson asked.

Nelda shook her head. "No, we didn't."

Nancy had a sudden hunch. She knew it was a wild idea, but she asked the customs man to pull the brass trimmings off the mystery trunk.

"That's one place we didn't examine," she said. "It's possible something is hidden under them."

Despite Otto August's protest the customs official took a chisel from his pocket and slowly raised one of the brass trimmings. There was nothing under it.

"This is preposterous!" August shouted. "I insist you stop wrecking my trunk!"

The customs man paid no attention. He deftly inserted the chisel under the second brass binding. As it fell off, an exquisite diamond bracelet came with it!

Nelda picked it up and turned it in her hands. "This is the one!" she cried out. "The one I was accused of stealing. Oh, Nancy, now I've been exonerated."

Otto August's face had become very pale and his friend was so weak he had to sit down on a nearby packing box. Nancy examined the tag on the bracelet. It was from a Johannesburg jeweler! She showed it to the FBI and customs officials.

Carson said, "This is the most important find we've made in a long time. We'll dub it the finger-language gang heist."

"These people also broke into our cabin and wrecked it," Nancy said. "And they threw Nelda and me overboard two nights ago."

August and his companion did not confess, but they did not deny the accusation either.

"Just tell me one more thing," Nancy asked the jewel thief. "On deck one day I picked up another part of a finger language message, 'Crew can help find necklace.' Whom did you refer to?"

August looked thoroughly beaten. "That had nothing to do with the *Winschoten*," he mumbled, but would say no more.

At this moment Rod Havelock walked up to the group. He asked Mr. Carson to accompany him to the captain's quarters. "We'll have to get the jewels and the documents out of his safe," Rod said, "and turn them over to the customs people."

"Of course," Carson replied.

Nancy turned to the FBI men. "I suppose this is all the proof you need to let us go?"

"Certainly. And let me commend you on having done a terrific job, Miss Drew."

The men said good-by and left just as Otto August and his friend were led away. A police officer went to collect the other luggage of the two men, who would be taken to headquarters.

Nancy's trunk was now examined along with her friends' luggage and okayed. A few minutes later the girls followed two porters who were wheeling their bags to the exit.

Directly on the other side of the visitors' fence stood three smiling boys, Ned, Burt, and Dave!

The girls received warm hugs and kisses, then Nelda was introduced. She said, "You boys are very lucky to have such marvelous girls as friends. They have done me a tremendous favor and cleared me of a false-theft charge, and they captured two criminals."

Ned laughed. "This doesn't surprise me in the least," he said. "Wherever Nancy goes, intrigue follows."

"I hope we will see one another soon," Nelda said. "But now I must leave you. I see relatives over there who have come to meet me."

Nancy, Bess, and George were sorry to see Nelda go. Would they ever have such an exciting time again with a roommate who started out as a stranger to them?

It was not long, however, before Nancy and her

friends were involved in another case, later called *Mystery at the Moss-Covered Mansion.*

As the young people walked toward the new Nickerson station wagon, Nancy said, "There's only one thing we haven't been able to find out."

"What's that?" Bess asked.

"Who ripped the stickers off August's trunk?"

"Maybe they came off in handling," George suggested.

"I doubt that," Nancy said. "Usually they're pasted on quite firmly. But I have a theory. What do you think about this? The two trunks are standing in the loading area. Along comes someone with mischief on his mind. He sees the similarity in the luggage and figures if he takes the stickers off he can cause some confusion."

"But then why did he remove them from one trunk and not the other?" George asked.

"Perhaps he was interrupted and had to run off."

"That's possible," George agreed. "And whom do you suspect?"

For a moment there was silence, then all three girls broke out in laughter. "Young Bobby. Who else?" Nancy chuckled.

"And you're right! Ha, ha!" said a little boy's voice as the mischievous youngster ran past them, swinging his skateboard.